The Grass Widow

By

D.A. Chadwick

The Grass Widow: A Civil War Tale
by D.A. Chadwick
3rd Edition © 2023 by WordMerchant Publishing
ISBN: 979-8-9872959-1-5
Library of Congress Control Number: 2023902567

Printed in the United States of America

**Dedicated to those women both known and unknown who fought in the Civil War disguised as men. A few are named below.**

Mary and Molly Bell
Privates Tom Parker and Bob Morgan of the 47th North Carolina Infantry

Frances Clalin
Missouri cavalry and artillery units

Sarah Edmonds
Private Franklin Thompson of the 2nd Michigan Volunteers

Jennie Hodgers
Private Albert D.J. Cashier of the 95th Illinois Infantry Regiment, Co G

Sarah Rosetta Wakeman
Private Lyons Wakeman of the 153rd Regiment New York State Volunteers

Mary Owens
John Evans

Satronia Smith Hunt
Iowa regiment

Mary Stevens Jenkins
Pennsylvania regiment

Albert D.J. Cashier   Co. G 95th Illinois Regiment
She lived her entire life as a man. Birth name is unknown.

# Chapter One

## 1861 Washington County, Tennessee

Mildred Carter made her way quickly down the narrow rail that plunged suddenly straight down for ten feet, and then curved around a grassy field where several cows grazed. The animals paid no attention to the white haired old woman who was as much a part of the landscape as the rocks and trees. She had often run or walked the rugged path between her place and that of her daughter, Jane Erwin, to tend the sick or eat a good meal. This evening Mildred looked forward to being served as she had spent the last week nursing the Cutter family back to health and was exhausted from the ordeal. Actually, it was just the wife and five children who had taken the gripe, but Wayne Cutter was as worthless as tits on a boar hog and could be counted on to help no one but himself. He spent most of his time cultivating corn liqueur and Millie could not recall the last time the man had worked.

As she crossed the clearing, the Erwin place came into view in the shallow valley below. Her son-in-law, Bill Erwin, led two large Belgian horses into a corral where they eagerly went for the hay piled in the center. Mildred went past the barn to the pump some fifty feet from the house to wash up. She had the notion that one ought to not go from a sick house to a well one without cleansing the hands, though the scientific world was years away from discovering germs as the cause of disease. The old healer had simply noticed that those living in clean, well ventilated houses suffered less illness and recovered faster.

Bill closed the corral gate and made his way across the barnyard while greeting his mother-in-law with, 'Hi, Grandma." Everyone in the county called Mildred Carter Grandma as she had either seen most of them born or helped them give birth or cured some ailment for them.

"I know Wayne was a big help with them kids." Bill said with a flat tone, knowing what her response would be and enjoyed giving her a hard time.

"I suspect there are slugs in this world with more ambition and sailors that drink less." Mildred worked the lye soap into her strong, rough hands. Bill chuckled. "I should know by now when you're baiting me, Mr. Erwin."

Bill laughed a she threw two handfuls of cool water onto his sweaty face. "Somebody has to keep you on your toes old woman!" He blotted his face and hands with the towel draped over the pump handle then passed it to Mildred.

"Yes, lord knows with my easy, soft life I could lose my edge." She hung the towel up to dry then shoved her hands into the pockets of her apron.

As they walked to the house Bill placed his big, warm hand on the middle of her back. Mildred often counted her blessings at having Bill Erwin for a son-in-law. Bill's brothers were fond of the drink and she was very grateful that Jane had not chosen of them to marry.

The Erwin house was a two-story box of a place with a wrap around porch. It had been white some years ago. Food and clothing came before paint and there was rarely any money for extras, but the home was clean and roomy enough for its seven occupants. The one oddity was a piece of stained glass in the front door that Bethel Erwin had found in a burnt out church, or so she said. The nineteen year old woman was a unique individual and seemed to fear nothing and no one. Mildred shook her head in amusement at the thought of her wild granddaughter.

The interior of the house was filled with the aroma of fried chicken and fresh bread, which aroused hunger pangs in Carter as she made her way through the living room to the enormous kitchen table. Jane placed a large platter of chicken in the center of the table and smiled at her mother and husband.

The noise level during dinner was controlled and the five children well behaved. Joe, the oldest at age twenty-two, was married and lived up on the mountain near Grandma Carter. Of the remaining children, Bethel was the oldest, then George at seventeen. Joy was fifteen, Ed nearly thirteen and Ellen just ten. The conversations began light then turned to the hot topic of secession by the southern states since the attack on Fort Sumner that April 1861. Bill was against it and thought the rich slave owners were playing the poor for fools, but such talk was dangerous. Bethel and George were excited by the aspect of war and paid little heed to the reasons behind it, which frustrated Bill whose grandfather was killed during the War of 1812. Joy, the studious one with wire spectacles stated that she thought the coming war was about state's rights.

"I have no problem fighting for what is right, but this war is about the rich not wanting to do their own damned work." Bill piled the mashed potatoes onto his plate then made a hole in the like a little volcano for gravy. "Most people here that I know have no use for secession or slavery, hell, I never knew anybody rich to own any! But you got to be careful with your talk, cause you never know who might be listening. The reality is that the rest of the state is siding with the Confederacy and we have to live here."

"It's going to happen sooner or later. They're gonna vote for secession and you know that new Yankee president ain't gonna stand for it." George tore into a chicken breast with gusto. The mere thought of being a soldier threw light on his boring existence in the Tennessee hills. "I'll join up with the Confederacy when the time comes."

"The war is no joke son. People die and don't be so thrilled with the possibility of it." Jane sliced pieces of bread and passed them around the table.

"Is there gonna be a war daddy? Cause I don't like fightin'." Ellen's large brown eyes looked like those of a fawn search for its mother.

"Yeah there is and I'm gonna kick some Yankee butt!" George tickled his little sister.

"You got that much energy you can help me clear some more land." Bill's lips slid into a crooked grin. "Bethel, ain't you got anything to say tonight?" He noticed that his oldest daughter seemed to be in some deep thought and she was just as riled up about events as George.

Bethel's smoky gray eyes lingered on some point on her plate and she had yet to take a bite. She had something to say alright, but wasn't about to announce those thoughts to the world. If there was going to be a war Bethel had every intention of being in it. "George is right. Trouble is brewing and Tennessee is going to jump into the middle of it sooner or later."

"Too bad you can't join up, Bethel. You shoot better'n me!" George shoveled mash potatoes and corn into his mouth and was told to slow down by his mother.

Mildred Carter studied her granddaughter's sudden change of mood and wondered if it meant anything or was just another of Bethel's dazed moments. The girl had many of them, but Mildred thought little of it as George was the same way. Both of them had creative natures with George being a musician and Bethel an artist, so their odd personalities were expected. But Bethel had a sadness to her that her brother did not and it seemed to make her soul just a bit older than it should be.

"No more talk of war now. I just spent a week with a sick, feudin' family and I want to hear some happy noises!" Grandma Carter raised her eyebrows and stuck out her hand for the plate of chicken.

"How long did ya nurse the Cutter's?" Bill asked.

"A week and I swear Wayne Cutter is worthless as tits on a boar hog." The kids giggle at her response.

"Mom!" Jane interjected trying to keep a smile off her face. "Well, he always has been and his daddy before him."

"Just Cluny and the kids got the gripe, but damned if he would lift a finger to help out." Mildred cut into a breast and watched the steam roll out of the meat.

"Now, Wayne's too busy nursin' that corn liqueur, Grandma!" Bill laughed.

"Well, corn liqueur must be ailing all the time cause a right fair number of menfolk always think it need tending." Mildred peered at him over her gold-framed glasses.

"Old Ma Cutter won't have to worry about her hubby running off to be a soldier. He'll stay right here and keep the home fires burning." Bill looked to his wife who rolled her eyes.

"Somebody has to tend that still now." Jane laughed and nudged her mother with left elbow.

"Brewin' mountain nectar takes some talent and you all shouldn't make fun of old Wayne." George remarked with a straight face.

"Just what do you know about makin' liqueur young man?" Mildred pointed at George with her fork.

"Better not know anything at all, right son?" Bill questioned the teenager.

"He knows as much about alcohol as he does girls." Bethel grinned and kicked her brother under the table which made the younger children laugh.

George's cheeks were full of mashed potatoes and it took him several seconds to swallow and respond. "Ha, ha. That's about as funny as the hind end full of buckshot you'll get the next time we go huntin'."

"You two stop. I made some apple pies, so everyone save some room" Jane wiped her mouth a she finished eating.

The napkins were made from an old bed sheet that had yielded a summer work shirt for Bill and a dozen of the large, striped napkins. The Erwin's were no strangers to hard times and knew how to make the most of what they had. Many of the mountain folk in eastern Tennessee were the same way and knew nothing of a lifestyle that would allow for owning slaves. For Bill and Jane the issue of secession was more about the rights of the states to govern themselves, not the right to enslave other human beings. The rest of the dinner conversation was kept to lighter subjects, which were easier on the digestion.

After the dishes were done up and the evening chores finished, Bethel and George sang an old favorite folk tune, Shady Grove, with George on the banjo and Bethel playing fiddle. Their voices blended well with his baritone and Bethel's alto. The family danced in the front yard, laughing and clapping for what would be the last time for a very long time.

It rained that night around midnight. Bethel Erwin woke up when the rain thumped the roof over her room. She got up and opened the windows that swung out from the center onto the back porch roof where Bethel often sat to think or sketch pictures. The rain smelled sweet and brought out the pine scent in the woods. The young woman never tired of studying the low clouds that hung over the valleys and wove their way through the hills giving the trees a smoky cast. The lightening lit up the steep ravine several yards from the house where a creek wound its way north through the forest. A haunting quiet fell with the rain and Bethel took a deep breath of the cool, wet air. She loved the rain and as far as Bethel was concerned it could rain four out of the seven days a week.

Something about the rain made all things possible and threw a romantic slant onto ordinary events. Rainy days depressed some people, but made Bethel happy to be alive. Her future was as cloudy as the night sky, so Bethel grasped at every good feeling that warmed her heart. More than likely she would end up taking her grandmother's place as the local healer and midwife, but the prospect did not thrill her. It had not gone unnoticed in the area that Bethel had not married and seemed to have no interest in doing so either. She had gone on a few dates to please her parents, but hated every minute of it. In truth, Bethel wanted no part of being a wife and mother. She was jealous of her brothers and the opportunities that awaited them. In 1861 there were few choices for women and at age nineteen Bethel hoped for some great event to intercede and provide an answer. A ripple of thunder rattled the glass in the windows then the clouds released a downpour. The rain was falling straight down so she left the windows open and went back to bed to crawl under a warm quilt.

It was still raining when Bethel milked the half dozen cows in the old barn just before dawn. There were gaps in the walls, but the roof did not leak, which was her father's main concern. The oldest of the cattle was named Cathy. She kept swinging her large head around to look at Bethel whenever she quit whistling or humming. Ellen had named the sweet natured Guernsey when she was five years old and the old cow behaved more like a big dog than livestock. The cow loved music and produced better when serenaded. When George placed his banjo outside, Cathy would stand next to the fence and tilt her head back and forth with the beat, a sight that was endearing as well as comical. The sun rise slowly crept through the open barn door easing the dark interior of the barn. Bethel turned off the lantern then stood up from the short milking stool. She rubbed the cow's back and received a soft rumble of contentment, then took the full pail of raw milk and poured it into a separator. While Bethel did not mind doing chores, it gave her too much time to think. What was going to happen in her adult life was a constant worry, but at least her parents had not forced to marry some clown against her will.

There were many girls Bethel had played with as a young child who had been promised to men shortly after their births. Their futures were well known with no uncertainties aside from the personalities of their husbands or whether childbirth would send them to the angels early in life. One of the saddest cases was the lot of her cousins Nancy Carter. Nancy was married off to Jason Harper who was fifteen years older than his bride and a Bible-thumping terror. He believed in keeping his young wife pregnant and began this chore nine months after the wedding. At age eighteen Nancy had four children with a fifth on the way. The cute, funny energetic playmate of Bethel's childhood looked now as if she were forty. Jason would not allow Nancy to associate with her spinster cousin as he thought that women committed a sin every time they menstruated. By his reasoning, Bethel had been depriving children of life since she was thirteen and an evil influence on his wife. Though Bethel missed her cousin's company, she could not tolerate the way Jason treated Nancy like she was livestock and was not beyond telling the old fart off.

Thirteen year old Ed Erwin stumbled into the barn appearing about as happy as any child does at six in the morning. It was his job to take the cows up to the pasture after the milking. Ed preferred hanging around Bethel more than his other two sisters who liked telling on him for every infraction. One could do most anything without worry of Bethel divulging the secret and more often than not, she would be involved in it.   She was easier to be around as Bethel liked dirty jokes and could swear as good as George and their cousin, Tim Carter.

"Think it's gonna rain all day? It's gonna be muddier then hell out there." Ed began to back Cathy out of the barn.

"That's true enough and it don't look like it's gonna quit anytime soon." Bethel carried fresh cream and milk to the door.

Jane Erwin made her children attend church until they were twelve then they could make their own choice in the matter. Bethel and George had elected not to go on Sunday mornings as those mornings were best spent enjoying nature on the creek bank, besides the Bible had a very limited vision of roles for women. None of them suited Bethel and she didn't care to sit and listen to how she should be subservient to men and be fruitful.

"Yeah, I kinda like the singin'. I hope he ain't too long winded today though. Sometimes that preacher don't know when to let up." Ed rubbed the old cow's nose then went to untie the other animals as they would follow Cathy out of the barn.

"Well, that preacher spends way too much time jawin' about Hell to suit me and most preachers seem bent on scaring the crap out of people. Don't see the point." At that moment the sky rumbled and Bethel grinned.

"Sure you don't need to go?" Ed laughed.

Bethel looked up the dark thunder heads and she shrugged her shoulders. "I figured if God don't like what I'm doin' I'll be struck dead and there ain't nothin' I can do about it. What's for breakfast?"

"Hot cakes and bacon. Smells real good too."

"You and Dad eat all that grub then nap in church, don't understand why Mom don't get sleepy though…well, see ya inside." The rain had accumulated on Bethel's old brown hat and ran down her back when she studied the clouds. A chill rolled down her spine.

Ed shook his head while trying to see through glasses spotted with water drops. He led the cow off up the hill to the pasture. Bethel grinned at the way his pants bagged at the rear-a hand-me-down from George. Being the youngest son of three Ed rarely wore virgin clothes.

"Better hurry up! It's gonna really let loose." She yelled on her way to the house.

It was still pouring two hours later when the family packed into the wagon for church. Ellen had the sniffles so she remained home with Grandma Carter. Jane talked George and Bethel into going as there was supposed to be a speaker that morning. Since it was raining they agreed as little else was possible in the way of activities.

Bill hovered under a blanket as the big Belgian pulled the wagon full of people down a heavily rutted road to the small church two miles west. The old plow horse seemed as enthusiastic as the driver who caught the rain head on as it soaked the blanket. In the back of the wagon under the cover Jane sat with her children. Joy had the perturbed look of a teenage girl with wet hair that hung limply around her face. She had already reminded Ed of the unfair convenience of being a boy. Jane appeared proper as always regarding the weather and she hummed a hymn as the rain pounded the tarp over the wagon bed.

Bethel and George wore bored expressions in their clean overalls and ironed shirts. She had refused to wear dresses long ago and her parents gave up trying to force her. Grandma Carter was her biggest ally and convinced them that to attempt to thwart Bethel's nature was a waste of time and would only serve to drive her away. Joy scowled at her sister whose hair never curled or frizzed. Bethel looked backed wide-eyed and shrugged. Ed laughed as George made devil's horns with his fingers. He stopped abruptly when his mother flatly stated that apparently they needed to attend church more often. Bethel jabbed his side for the infraction.

More than half the congregation forewent the morning services as evidenced by the few wagons and horses hitched to the rails outside the church. The well worn path to the church was a ribbon of mud and pooling water that most of the Erwin's maneuvered, except for Joy whose right foot slid out from under her. She landed in the reddish mud tainted by the iron ore in the soil, her light green skirt fluffed out around her like the petals of a huge flower. The sound of her behind slapping the mud made her parents turn suddenly.

Water flowed down the front of Bill's hat as he pointed at his fallen daughter. "That…is God's way of saying we should stay home when it's storming'!" The other children hoot and snicker.

"I can't go in like this!" Joy whined.

Ed giggled. "Well sit there long enough and you'll get a bath."

"That's enough, you two help your sister up." Jane held the door open as she addressed Bethel and George.

The preacher was the Reverend Tom Wilkes who had come to Washington County from Vicksburg, Mississippi. The preacher was sitting behind the podium with a stranger in a black suit, who Bill assumed was the guest speaker.

He was young, idealistic and knew nothing of hard times. While Wilkes wasn't the best minister Jane had ever heard, he was all they had and Jane figured that God had sent him to Tennessee to learn about plain folk. Bill was much less charitable in his assessment of the balding, chinless man who he found pompous and boring. Wilkes was not beyond using the pulpit to push his political views either. Though he had not come out and said it, Wilkes approved of the butchering done by John Brown in Kansas. Bill was of the opinion that there were those in the world who liked to maim and murder and if they could put a cause behind it all the better. The Reverend was passionate and on fire all the time, which to Bill only added up to trouble. It was men such as Tom Wilkes who stirred people into actions good and bad.

Bill did fall asleep in the pew as he did every Sunday, but that morning Jane nudged him awake. Bethel and George sat up straight as their father woke up. The tall man stood up as Wilkes introduced him as Captain Merriweather. He appeared to be around thirty with black hair and brown eyes and a freshly shaved chin. "My name is Michael Merriweather and I'm a lawyer from Kentucky. I know that the sentiment of most of your fine state tends to be Confederate, but Reverend Wilkes tells me that some of you are pro Union." His tone was calm and he discreetly searched the crowed for signs of hostility. "I am recruiting for the 2nd Tennessee. This is a time to follow your conscious and make a stand. I know that won't be easy for some of you as there are strong opinions about what is right and wrong here, but if anyone is interested I will be at the train station in Johnson City for the next two mornings. I'm no military man, however, I worked my way through college as a supervisor in a coal mine and I know a few things about leading men. I have no problem admitting that I don't know everything and will prize the advice of my career army sergeants. Hope to see some of you there."

The congregation mumbles and whispers with the talk of war. Ed's eyes widen with excitement as the captain nods politely to the parishioners while walking down the center aisle out of the church. The boards groaned as each boot made contact with the bare wood floor. Joy no longer seemed concerned with her wet hair with the reality of war staked out before them. Wilkes rushed back to the podium.

"Friends, we must all stand for what is right. No man has a right to own another, regardless of his skin color. I can't tell y'all what to do…"

Abner Speaks, a thin man of seventy, stands up holding his hat in both hands. His wife Emma appears surprised as Abner is usually timid. "Damn right! "It don't matter one bit what we think around here as Tennessee is goin' to withdraw from the Union and anybody that sides with the Yanks is gonna regret it."

The Speaks were an older couple who lived on the outskirts of Limestone, which lay on the tracks of the East Tennessee, Virginia and Georgia Railroad. Eastern Tennessee would be a hot bed in the up coming conflict as it was filled with bridges and tracks that link the eastern side of the Appalachian Mountains with the west.

"He's right you know. We live in Limestone where the railroads intersect and I'm afraid for our lives. Bad times are coming." Emma's voiced cracked with worry.

"I have to agree with Abner. We have more to consider than who is right or wrong. We live here and it won't be real safe here for anyone who backs the Union." Bill remained seated, but turned right so that he could face the rest of the congregation.

Reverent Wilkes stepped around to the front of the podium with his arms spread wide. "If we stand together we need not be afraid. Please, good people, help me made a stand."

"I didn't come here to listen to this political trash! I cam here to worship the Lord, not to have some high falooten fancy lawyer try to talk my grandsons into dying' for his cause!" Sally Brookfield straightened her ample bosom as she nudged her daughter, son-in-law and two grandsons out of the pew. The congregation mumbles and nods in agreement.

"Mrs. Brookfield, I mean no disrespect, but the righteous must have a voice!" Wilkes pleaded with his hands together as if he were praying.

"I've lost a husband and three babies in this life and I'll not lose even one more of my family for you or anyone else." Sally and her clan left the church in a huff. The other members also get up to leave.

"No, please don't go." The preacher nearly whined in desperation.

Jane Erwin walked over to Wilkes and put a hand on his right arm. "Don't get us wrong, Reverend, but we've lived here a long time and know when and how to make a stand. Dangerous times are ahead for us all."

It was raining harder as the Erwin's were leaving church. Jane sat up front under the blanket with her husband, neither of then saying anything but both thinking that they could soon lose their sons. George would join up for sure and Joe might even though he would leave behind a wife and three children. Jane peeked through the canvas wagon top to see Ed smiling and pretending to shoot his sisters. George and Bethel salute each other and their siblings. The romance of war was a deadly lure for the young.

## Chapter Two


Eastern Tennessee in the spring of 1861 was fertile, mountainous, iron rich, full of rivers and rail connections to the eastern side of the Appalachians. The farmers of the east owned no slaves and tended to side with the Union, but most of the state was in favor of the Confederacy. The Reverend Wilkes was one of many who believed that God was furious with those that enslave others and the war was punishment for that sin. It would not end until enough blood had been spilled.

While it was a fearsome thought for Bill and Jane Erwin, it was a promise of untold adventure for George Erwin who walked down the muddy streets of Longmire with his sister Bethel. In his excitement about the coming war he had not noticed that she was unusually sullen and without comment. She was staring at a piece of paper announcing the formation of the 2nd Tennessee Infantry for the Confederate States Army. George and their cousin, Tim Carter, planned to join up in Nashville even though George was a few months shy of eighteen. Bethel had ripped it off the side of the post office after they had fetched the mail for their mother.

"You ought not to have done that. Other people might want to read it."

"I could do this, damn it isn't fair." Her blonde bands swung to and fro in time with her determined stride.

George read from the poster. "Wanted, all able-bodied MEN to join the ranks of the 2nd Tennessee C.S.A."   He snickered. "Maybe you could follow us and do our laundry." George laughed loudly when she punched him.

"I could whip your ass and any other boy's around here!" Bethel balled up the paper in her right hand and gave it a toss toward the dry goods store.

"You and what army?" George began to dance around like a boxer throwing punches in the air.

The dark frown on her face turned slowly upward on one side. "The 2nd Tennessee."

"Think we need to stop by Doc Nichols cause you ain't well."

"Why not? How many times have I been taken for a fella when you, me and Tim was huntin'?"

"You cain't. No way, there is no way. You'd have to live with nothin' but men and sooner or later somebody would find out." George shook his head at the sheer absurdity of the idea.

"So what? I'd just go back home then wouldn't I?" Bethel's gray eyes danced with delight.

"If ya live that long. Pa would tear the hide right off my backside if I helped you run off and join the army. Damn Bethel, you do beat all." George already knew that the three of them would jump the train for Nashville. He really could not blame her for being mad at being left out and Bethel would do it with or without his help. At least they would all be together.

"Wonder if I go and join up with the Union?  You know I can shoot better'n you?" Bethel teased as she walked backwards with her hands buried deep in the pockets of her worn overalls.

"I'd rather join the Union army, but that wouldn't do for Ma and Pa if I did that. There's too many hot heads around here to chance it. I know Pa's right about the slave owners gettin' us poor folk to do their fightin'. You done some pretty wild things Bethel, but this ain't no game." George bit his bottom lip in thought.

"And so could you and Tim...why is it worse cause I'm a girl?" She shrugged her shoulders to accent the question and her brother kicked a rock in response.

A woman and her two daughters emerged from the dry goods store; their chatting filled the air. Bethel's lip curled upward in a sneer. It was Pam Neukirk, her mother and young sister. The Neukirks in Georgia owned slaves and plantations. Pam thought that having rich relatives automatically made her superior to the Erwins, especially George who had a crush on the pretty brunette. Bethel had little use for the uppity teenager or her equally smug brother, Brandon.

In school the Neukirk kids always had nice notebooks and plenty of pencils and their clothes were never patched, unlike the Erwin bunch that often had to make do with second or third hand-me-downs. There had been more then one time that Bethel had sent Pam home with a good sized rip down her pretty new dress and a shiner to match. Jane Erwin had made Bethel milk the Neukirk cows for a week to pay for one dress.

"Bethel and George, well how's your mother and father these days?" Deirdre Neukirk had wide hips that were further accented by the snug dress she wore. She had the air of an old gray goose as she waddled slowly toward the Erwins.

"They are just fine Mam, thank for asking." George tilted his head like an English gentleman.

Pam wore a dark blue dress with tiny white roses throughout the material. She studied George from his old boots to the crown of his weathered hat, and then met his eyes. "You know, Brandon will be joining up as soon as he finishes this semester at the university. They're organizing a regiment over in Greene County and Sam Powell has offered my brother an officer's commission. I don't suppose that you'll be going with the farm work and all?"

George cast Bethel a warning glance as she stifled a snort. "I've been considering military experience, even though my Pa needs the extra hand."

"We'll do our share; don't you worry none about that!" Bethel pulled her hands from the deep pockets and crossed her arms.

"Why, I was not implying that you would not, Bethel Erwin. In fact, you should sign up as you are surely meaner than any boy I ever did meet."

"Pam, that is not very lady like and very impolite!" Mrs. Neukirk corrected her daughter.

"Guess Pam just brings out the devil in me, Mam. I don't pay her no mind." Bethel replied in a cool tone which made Pam glad that their school days were over.

"Well, you tell your parents that I asked after them." Deidra placed a gloved hand on the head of her seven year old daughter and turned the child in the opposite direction.

George tipped his old hat as the Neukirks walked casually down the muddy street, avoiding the puddles. He tried so hard to meet Pam's approval that it made Bethel nearly puke. There were some people in this world that would never measure up to certain standard and the Erwins were just such a group. It was a fact of life that was not easily changed and Bethel saw no reason to kiss anyone's ass, especially that of Pam Neukirk.

It was no task to maintain a petite figure, soft hands and a delicate disposition when one's father was an executive with the railroad and a servant girl took care of any unpleasant chores. Those that wore nice, expensive clothes were never exposed them to the elements or the rigors of farm work. Women such as Deidra and Pam Neukirk pretended to float above the menial aspects of life, yet the hems of their skirts drug through the mud the same as any slave woman's.

"Like they really care how our parents are doing." Bethel looked after the trio with scorn.

"Oh Beth, don't be such a horse's butt." George watched the sway of the hoop skirt as Pam strolled down the street.

"I think your brain has dropped about two feet down." Bethel laughed.

"You talk big for someone who wants my help joining the army." George turned back around as they started out of town for home. Longmire was a little over two miles from the Erwin farm. Suddenly George began to act prissy and spoke in a mocking tone. "Brandon's gonna be an officer."

"Wouldn't just love to throw dog shit on his starchy white shirt?" Bethel reached into the top pocket of the overalls and retrieved a red gumball that she popped into her mouth. "Maybe we'll run into him at some battle and fix his fancy wagon. He's such an ass."

"You're serious?" You're serious?" George stared at his sister.

"Hell yeah, the look on Brandie's face would be priceless." Her jaw muscles worked hard to break into the shell of the gum, which mumbled her words.

"No, idiot, serious about the army."

"You should know me by now." Bethel replied.

# Chapter Three

Bethel and Mildred ascended the steep hill to the Clutter place on a beautiful cool morning.  Wildflowers bloomed among the tall grass before the thick trees conquered the meadow. The two women were strong and healthy from years of climbing the steep terrain and caring for the sick and disabled.  Mildred was slightly slower and breathed more heavily, slight compensations for a woman with fifty years on the planet longer than her granddaughter.

"I don't know how you do it, Grandma. You are so patient. I just wanna smack Wayne upside his fat head for the unkindness he shows his wife and children." Bethel frowned. "I need to see the world. Nothing will ever change around here."

Mildred pulled her skirts up higher as they approached the top of the ridge. "I know you better than you think, Bethel. I also understand more than you think cause I've seen a lot in this old world.  Ain't nothin' in this world wiser than an old widow, except maybe a grass widow."

When Bethel seemed confused, Mildred stopped near an old stump. "You can make your way without a man is my point. I ain't sayin' it will be easy for you, but it could be a damned sight easier than marrying somebody you don't want to live with. Your grandfather has been dead twenty years and I done just fine."

Bethel jammed her sweaty hands into her pockets. "I just want something different, out of these hills! Oh, I don't know exactly. What's a grass widow?"

"A grass widow is a young woman who just lost her husband. Usually she has a small child. She's in a sort of limbo with no real place in this world, kind of like you, Beth. She's always outside looking in. You have to be true to yourself, whatever that truth may be. I seen too many people sick in the heart from being who they aren't."

The teenager looked back out over the valley to the Erwin house in the distance. It was beautiful there and the sweet smells of the rain, pine trees and honey suckle made her heart sing, but some sadness, some sense of incompleteness fill her soul. She had to find that missing part or grow old and shriveled before her time.

"I'd like to go to school. In New York City or some place."

Mildred patted Bethel's shoulder as they continued on the path to the Cutter house. "You can do anything you want to do; I don't doubt that!"

The interior of the Clutter cabin is messy, dishes piled up on the table and in the washing tub in the corner. There was no sign of Grandma Carter's presence a week earlier. Cluny is still obviously weak from her illness and unable to care for children or clean. She is wrapped in an old quilt in rocking chair made by her father. Several small children laugh and squeal as they run about the three room cabin. One of them answers the door to reveal Bethel and her grandmother.

Cluny smiles slightly, but is embarrassed by the appearance of her home. Her hair is unruly and dark circles draw attention from her usually bright blue eyes. Grandma Carter asks if she has been drinking the medicinal tea as ordered. She answers slowly with a heavy drawl.

"As often as I can get up. I'm still sa tired out."

"Can't Wayne help ya out with the kids and all?" Mildred asked fully knowing the answer.

"Well, now Grandma, that's woman's work."

One of the children ran into Mildred. "Why don't you kids go on outside now and I'll visit with yer Ma?" The children, two boys and a girl flung open the front door and take off amid laughing and squeals of delight.

Bethel cleared off a pile of dishes from the table as her grandmother filled a kettle with pump water then lit the stove.

"I'm so embarrassed.   This place is a filthy mess."

"Don't fret about that now. You just make sure you drink my tea if you do nothin' else. I hear that rumble startin' up again in yer chest and I just got that healed up Cluny Carter!" Mildred waved a finger at the sickly woman.

The bellowing of Wayne Cutter telling his brats to keep it down for his planned nap could be heard through the open door. Bethel looks to her grandmother as the heavy sound of his footsteps could be heard clumping across the warped, weathered boards of the porch. He stands in the threshold; the gaping sides of his overalls fail to control the rolls of blubber struggling for release. Wayne is drunk and cradling a jug in his left arm. He bellows at his wife about the condition of the house.

"Now you listen to me, Wayne Cutter! Cluny is very sick and unless you want to raise these young'uns by yerself, I suggest you help her out around here." Mildred said in a manner more graceful than her actual thoughts.

"There ain't nothin' wrong with her 'cept she's no damned good for nothin'"
He looks to his ailing wife with no trace of pity.

Bethel's lip curls. "Think yer talkin' about yerself."

Wayne smiles. "You need to learn yer place little girl. What ya need is a husband to give ya a good beatin' ever so often."

"You'll not talk to her that way. If ya want Cluny well so she can wait on yer lazy ass, then you'd best go back up that hill and tend that still!" Mildred's cheeks flushed with anger.

Cutter snorted. "There ain't nothin' wrong with her, she's just too damned stupid for livin'."

"Honey, I'm almost better. I just need ta drink the tea like she said." Cluny pleaded in a weak voice; the circles under eyes appeared to get darker with the exertion.

Wayne storms over to the rocking chair and pulls Cluny out of it. She falls to the floor and erupts into a coughing fit. He slapped her on the head prompting Mildred to step in between the couple just time for Wayne's ham of a fist land on her back. The blow knocked her into wood pile. Bethel jumped up and kicked Cutter in the rib cage. He called her a female dog and groaned.

"I'd kick ya in yer Johnny, but I ain't got time to look fer it." Bethel shouted at the man still bent over.

Mildred scrambled from the cut wood and glared at Wayne. "Beth, get on outta here now. Cutter you hurt my granddaughter and I'll pickle ya in yer own damned juices!"

Cluny Cutter got to her knees and through a sharp sounding cough told Wayne to get the hell out. She struggled not to flinch while he contemplated her tone of voice.

"I'll go this time. Only cause you got a fever in yer brain. That's the only reason you better be talkin' to me like that!"

Bethel stands outside near an old deformed oak while the children covered their mouths to muffle laughter. Wayne tripped over a wooden toy and fell on his face. He swore at the children who had obviously heard it before. Cutter studied Bethel who glared at him with steely eyes. She noticed that one of the straps on his overalls had torn loose and Cutter grew angrier as she tried to keep his clothes on. The jug of mash spilled onto the ground so he let go of his pants to grab it.

His huge hairy belly rolled out as Wayne kneeled in the dirt. "Ain't you got nothin' to say now, wise ass?"

Bethel snickered. "You and yer happy clan just helped me make a big decision. Guess I should be glad I came along today."

The obese man struggled to his feet, breathing heavily. "If 'n you wasn't a female…"

"You'd what? It ain't like you got a problem smackin' women around. Do yer wife a favor and drown yerself in that still up yonder."

The youngest girl stayed close to Bethel and grabbed her hand. The entire family was under fed except for Wayne who had enough fat to survive an Alaskan winter with no provisions at all. Bethel watched the huge man wander off toward the path cut into the woods near the house leading to his still. He disgusted her as did the condition of the ramshackle house and miserable existence of the woman inside. Never would she ever live that way and never would Bethel ever be forced into marriage.

Mildred emerged from the cabin and stood on the porch with her hands on her hips. "I need all you children to help your mother. Ya hear me? She is not going to live if she don't get some rest. I don't mean to be cruel, just statin' the facts. Come on Bethel, we got more stops to make."

The other patients consisted of a pregnant woman, a teenage boy with an ear ache and an old man with the trots. All would live and continue their wretched lives in the hills, passing the hopelessness onto one generation after another. Bethel was depressed at the end of the day and more determined an ever to find another life.

# Chapter Four

Captain Merriweather stood alone on the platform at the Johnson City train station in civilian clothes, glancing periodically at his pocket watch. He never thought coming there was a good idea, but reverend Wilkins had convinced him that many were loyal to the Union in the area. That might be true; however, most would not have the courage to flaunt it. Merriweather paced as he waited for the train. He cut a dignified image as his three piece suit hung perfectly on a thin frame.

In the trees across the tracks from the station three pairs of eyes studied the Union officer. Bethel, George and their cousin, Tim Carter watched as the disappointed Merriweather bided his time until the next train.

"Ain't no way anybody was gonna show up, got guts though." Bethel peered from behind the trunk of a large pine tree.

George stood behind the thick pine branches of the same tree. "That preacher should have his ass kicked bringin' him to church like that. He coulda got the man killed."

Tim nodded in agreement; his mouth full of chaw. "Men like that don't think before they open their big mouths. They got their causes and that's all they care about."

"The train to Nashville leaves tomorrow morning. Let's jump it when it stops at Shucker's Bend?" Bethel looked to her brother and cousin for approval.

Tim nodded and spit at the same time. George made a face. "How can you chew that nasty shit?"

Carter walked over to George and put a hand on his shoulder. "That's the difference between a man and a boy, son!" Tim feigned pain as George punched him and the arm. "We could ride the train like everbody else if 'someone' didn't feel inclined to go."

"You can try talkin' to her. I give up." George shrugged his shoulders

"I'm joinin' up one way or another. Ya all can go sign up with Brandon Neukirk and I'll go ta Nashville." Bethel's tone was irritable.

"I already tried talkin' her into doin' the troop laundry and she about kicked my ass." George added as the sound of a train whistle made them look of to the left.

"Poor Captain Merriweather is goin' home with no soldier boys." Bethel lamented.

George stepped back from the branches and shouted as the train squealed to a halt. "He's lucky to be leavin' with his head attached."

*************

That evening at the Erwin house, Jane mended clothes near an oil lamp that she shared with Joy in the living room. Joy would read anything and everything she could find and often borrowed books from the school teacher, Miss Rankin. George and Bethel lay on their stomachs playing checkers near the fireplace across from their father who cleaned his hunting rifle. The atmosphere was quiet with the younger children already upstairs in bed.

George turned on his side toward his mother. "Ma, we saw the Neukirks today and Mrs. Neukirk asked after you and Pa."

Bill made a grunting sound that Jane ignored. "That was considerate of her." Her husband had little use for those with too much money and the need to flaunt it, especially during hard times.

"And they just had to tell us that Brandon is join' up as an officer." Bethel remarked as she took several of George's black pieces.

"That little bastard never did a hard day's work in his life. You mark my words, with leaders like him that war will not soon end!" Bill laid his rifle down to roll a cigarette.

"Well, I wouldn't fight under him." George announced matter-of-factly like an old soldier.

"You ain't fightin' at all! Not til they make ya." Bill Erwin's voice was deep with the fear of losing his son.

George made a face at his sister when he noticed her moves. "Everybody round here is gonna say I'm some kind of pansy, Pa."

Bethel chuckled. "Certain snotty girls you mean?"

"Aw, yer just jealous of them pretty blonde curls." George smirked as he took two over red checkers.

"I envy Pam Neukirk like I would a pregnant cow."

Jane peered over her reading glasses. "Will you two stops?"

Bill took several puffs on the cigarette then looked down on his son. "I wouldn't waste my dreams on the likes of her. You will never have enough money, son."

"She's got good qualities."

"I've seen her qualities, ALL of 'em!" Bethel got up and pranced around the room pretending to hold a parasol. "Oh George, would you throw yourself over that little old mud puddle for me, and then swat the flies offa me?"

Bill tried not to laugh and as called her down. "Bethel, don't torment yer brother like that….yer day is coming ya know."

When Bethel rolled her eyes Jane added, "You are not immune to thought of romance dear."

Bethel stops and appears sober. "Then I shall a cure!"

"You remember that old story, the one about that Scotsman?" Bill asked his wife who nodded. "Old Tandy the Scott, that's what they called him when my father was a boy. Got his heart broke by some gal back east and swore to never date again. He didn't neither, but musta got lonely cause he would go up to that peak across the way and play his pipes late at night."

Joy, who loved to hear stories, asked what became of him.

"Went up there one stormy night and was playing them pipes as the rain poured and the thunder rolled, almost like he was challenging the Almighty. Lightening bolt struck him dead and my granddad buried him up there." Bill smiled as he recalled hearing the tale as a boy.

Later that night a cool breeze blew threw Bethel's window. She climbed out onto the roof and looked to the peak high over the creek, the image of a Scotsman's silhouette not hard to envision. The moon was bright and full and the air full of sweet pine. Such nights made Bethel long for some unknown place where she was to fulfill her destiny. She had no idea of where she was supposed to be. She only knew that it was far from Longmire, Tennessee.

# Chapter Five

The three of had jumped the train as it stopped for water at Shucker's Bend. The interior of the box car was filled with large wooden crates. George had pushed two of them out from the wall to form an enclosed area where the three runaways could hide from the Pinkertons, who were not known for kindness and compassion.

Bethel appeared much like her brother and cousin with her lean frame and small breasts. Years of hunting and farming had developed her body much like theirs. It would not be so hard to pretend she was a man to enlist.

"I'll bet Pa is about ready to skin our butts about now." George chewed a piece of grass he'd pulled when they jumped the train.

Bethel listened to the creaking of the crates as they kept time with the clacking of the tracks. "Naw, I got Ed to do our chores for us so we'd have a good head start."

"Well, once they realize we've gone off to do something honorable they'll get over it I'm sure." Tim dropped his chin down on his chest, his big brown hat providing some shade for a nap. He had black hair and swarthy skin that never seemed to sunburn.

"Our Pa don't think fightin' fer the south is all that honorable. I just wanna get into the battle is all. I got no cause to speak of." George spit out a piece of grass.

"Me neither. I'm just so bored in them damned hills I could croak." Beth stood up and hopped over a box. "I got to stretch my legs, boys."

"You said it, alright. I got no desire to be a damned plowboy my whole life. All ya do as a farmer is bust yer ass day in and day out to be poor." Carter lamented from under the hat.

George joins Bethel in the center of the car to walk the sleep out of his stiff legs. It was hard to keep balance in the rolling car until half an hour later the train began to slow down.

"They must need to take on water. You get back behind the boxes and I'll watch out fer them railroad detectives."

George crawled back over into the hideout. "Just let one of them Pinkerton son-of- a-bitches throw me off this train!"

Bethel peered through the slit in the sliding door as the car came to a stop. The engine halted next to a wooden water tower. A man emerged from a small shack near the tower and laughed at something the engineer shouted from the doorway of the engine. She looked back the other direction and saw a brakeman in the distance walking the tracks inspecting the rail car couplings. Cursing to herself she hopped up on the box and gently dropped to the other side. The three of them cast nervous glances to each other as they waited for the man to past by. Tim tapped his foot and was elbowed by George.

The brakeman stood outside the door, stretched his back then lit a match on the rail car door. He was an older man with sweat running down his face as he smoked a pipe for the short break. After a minute he strolled on up to the shack much to the relief of the stowaways inside.

Bethel silently let out a lung full of air as she stared at the roof the car. She turned to George and Tim sitting on the floor across from her, grinning mischievously.

"What the hell is so funny?" George whispered.

She looked to the wet spot in Tim's pants. George followed her eyes and saw that the urine had soaked the wood boards beneath him. He smiled broadly and shook his head in agreement when Bethel remarked that she sure would feel safe in the army with Tim around.

"Both of you just shut the hell up." Tim covered his pants with the wide brimmed hat.

A few days later on May 5, 1861 the trio wandered down the streets of Nashville in awe since they had never been to a city that size before. The streets are full of buggies, wagons and pedestrians. A band played under a gazebo in the park a few blocks from a saloon where the loud piano music and laughter leaked into the night air.

George licks his lips. "Wonder if we could...."

"We don't have enough money fer socializing." Tim stepped in front of George.

"Sounds like a good time though don't it?" Bethel asked as she strained to see what was going on inside.

The large windows framed the activity inside, which was a menagerie of card games, show girls and a fight between a short man and one rather big, angry one. The small man laughed and was soon thrown out of the swinging doors onto the wood walkway.

"Get out and stay out this time!" The saloon bouncer shouted.

The ejected man wore a three piece suit and flashed the three boys a toothy grin while climbing to his feet. He sported a dark brown mustache and goatee. Bethel thought he looked like a banker or some such type.

"Too much of a good time, huh?" Bethel grinned.

"You boys lost?" The stranger asked as he sized them up.

"We're signin' up fer the 2nd Tennessee tomorrow morning'". Tim announced solemnly.

"I've played a soldier a few times, but got no desire to study the role any closer. Name's Miles Harper." Harper extended his hand to each of them.

"Well, I'm George and you say you played a soldier? You're an actor then?"

"That I am and who are your friends?" Miles seemed to have a mischievous glint in his eye.

"I'm Tim and this is my cousin, Bethel."

Miles studied Bethel's face then nodded. "I got a small house in town, would you like to join me for a bite to eat, unless you all have other plans?"

The trio looked to each other then Bethel responds, "No, actually we don't."

"Follow me then!"

They strolled several blocks away from the noise and lights to a quieter section of town where neat two-story houses lined the streets. The spring air was cool and a hint of rain scented the air. Harper stopped before a cream colored house with a short white fence around the front yard. He bowed while opening the gate and bid them to enter. George chuckled at the fancy treatment.

Inside, Miles took off his jacket and vest and laid them over a red love seat then rolled up his sleeves. The living room was small with a fireplace on the east wall. The wall paper was white with thin pink lines and roses running vertically. Bethel was impressed as the Erwin's only had plain painted walls.

"I don't have much, but there's cheese, bread and strawberry jam. Oh and there's a jar of honey butter, a gift from an admirer." Harper grinned slyly. "Come on into the kitchen."

The four of them sat a square table with an oil lamp in the center. Harper laid out the food and some milk. "I could make coffee if you all would like it?" His guests declined saying the milk was fine. Miles sat down and began to cut slices of bread.

"You say you're joining the army tomorrow, all of you?" Harper accented all of you.

Bethel's face reddens a bit.

"Yeah, we're gonna give it a try anyways. We've done everything together since we was kids and we think we ought to stick together now too." George smeared jam onto his thick piece of white bread.

Miles smiles and winks at Bethel who responds with a question. "You ain't gonna give me away are ya?" Her heart pounded with dread.

Tim appears oblivious to the conversation as she munches a chunk of cheese. George and Bethel both watch Harper as he ponders an answer.

"We do what we have to do in this world and we don't always get dealt the cards we'd like. So, what do you do? Fold before the game starts or cheat a little?" Miles shrugged his shoulders.

George knitted his eyebrows in a frown." What do ya mean?"

Bethel runs her eyes over Harper's face. "How, I would never have known."

"I study people, all people and it doesn't hurt to be good with spirit gum either."

Tim stopped chewing "What the hell do ya do with that? What's that got to do with card playin'?"

George shakes his head and flicks Tim on the ear. "I wouldn't count on makin' general."

"I take acting very seriously, but the world doesn't take women very seriously. I like the exciting leading roles and there aren't many for females." Miles enjoyed being able to speak casually with the three teenagers. It did not happen often that Harper did not have to hide.

"Nobody knows, but how?" Bethel leaned closer to Miles.

"This is a delicate society we live in today. I am just a modest gentleman with a preference for privacy. My real name is Kim Miles. Would you MEN like a sip of scotch?"

Tim's face lit up. "Hell, yeah."

"Sure, might as well live while we can." George punched Bethel's shoulder.

Miles clapped her hands together and jumped up to grab a bottle of single malt scotch, another gift from a female admirer. "This is good. I don't get much company you know, it's too risky."

Tim belched. "Don't know what yer talkin' about but I'll sure share yer scotch."

"I think we should request to be in a different company, don't you George?"

"Well, he ain't the loudest owl in the tree, that's fer sure."

Later that night Bethel sat in front of an oval shaped mirror in her long underwear as Kim Miles trimmed Bethel's hair in a white nightshirt. As she cut the locks Miles put them in a box. She soon put the scissors down and reached for a jar of spirit gum on the dressing table sporting the mirror.

"We'll just put some of the gum over your lip like this…then start placing the hair along the top of your lip and work upward. That way it looks natural."

As Miles worked Bethel watched until she had a full mustache that hung down over her lip. The other woman then trimmed the excess.

"Damn, I can't believe it. But won't it come off, like when it rains?"

"No, spirit gum is hard to get off, but I'll give ya some to take with ya. You should probably have a beard too, so that nobody will find it strange that you never need to shave."

"I just can't believe it. I really look like a man. How long have you been living as Miles Harper?"

Kim sat the bed next to the dressing table. "Since I left home, guess it's been about ten years now. I didn't see any future for me in a traditional sense of the word. It actually hasn't been that difficult, 'cept I don't have many close friends."

"What about yer family?" Bethel watched the mustache move with her words.

"They don't know. I use the stage name of Miles Harper around here and when I visit home in New York I go as a woman. I think my grandmother suspects something, but she never says a word. I told them I work in the theater as a make up artist." Miles studied the make up job on her new friend and was pleased. "Give any thought to the name you're going to use?"

"Tandy Scott. There's an old grave in the hills back home with that name on it. Guess he got struck by lightening while playin' the bagpipes." She shrugged her shoulders.

Miles chuckled at the choice. "Let's work on that beard. I've made it for ten years pretending to be a man, so I think you can do it for a few months. Nobody thinks that war will last any longer. If you write me ever now and again I'll send ya more spirit gum. You can tell me all about yer war experiences."

"I sure will. Why did those men throw ya outta that saloon?"

A broad grin crossed Kim's face. "Ever now and then I go drinking and card playing to keep up the male image. I flirted with the wrong girl tonight. Funny thing is, the ladies seem to like e better'n the real men. One of these days I'm gonna get my ass kicked." She winked at Bethel who appeared amazed.

Bethel looked down at the pretty Persian style rug. "I didn't know what kind of life I was gonna have neither. The least objectionable was taking over for my grandmother as the healer. In the hills all a woman has to look forward to is a husband and a house full of brats. It's enough to make me want to throw myself into the Nolochucky River."

Miles rubs gum over Bethel's lower jaw and starts to layer hair for a beard. "I know the feeling dear. I damned well do. Anatomy condemns females to a kind of slavery. Cause even if ya do want the family routine, it's all ya ever gonna get and you got no right to ask for more. Men on the other hand can do whatever they want and still expect an old lady to wait on him and take care of the kids. No indeed, I would rather live ten years this way than forty being married to some son-of-a-bitch."

She turns Bethel's jaw the other direction to work on the far side. "Don't mind me. I could wail on all night about it."

"I'm just glad to know that I'm not the girl to ever feel like perch in a cornfield."

Miles let out a laugh. "Well, you're not and I suspect there'll be a fair amount of women joining the ranks with ya. Just make sure that ya make it through the war so ya can tell me war stories. And do write, soldier boy."

"My spellin' ain't so great, but I'd sure like to tell ya about my trials in army life."

Kim stepped back to admire her handiwork. "I'll be damned if ya don't make a better lookin' fella than me! Take a gander at yerself."

Bethel turns the stool back towards the mirror and a young man looks back at her. "My god, that's me?"

"You'll do find, Beth and ya have your brother and cousin to help ya. You just act like you're too bashful to do your business around others and take a bath in yer skivvies. You do just fine. And start using the name Tandy now. You are no longer Bethel Erwin, but Tandy Scott. It's very important that you get your mind right so you don't make mistakes."

Bethel had a long sleepless night worrying about being caught and life in the army if she was allowed to sign up. George was right when he said that all she had to do was to be herself. Except for the name and hairy face it was true, but Bethel was nervous about spending twenty four hours a day, seven days a week being surrounded by men. While her behavior had always made men her best friends, she had never actually pretended to be one of them. Miles Harper had fooled people for ten years, so she had evidence that women could live as men with none being the wiser. Tandy Scott would have to do the same.

## Chapter Six

The Nashville recruiting station was housed in an old store front with the faded name of the previous occupant still splayed across the wide window.  Inside were three men seated at a long table to serve the line of volunteers that snaked out into the street. Bethel surveyed the scene with eyes shielded by the wide brim of her hat, the beard and mustache made her appear older than her brother and cousin who squirmed with impatience at the long wait.
"Shit, it sure is takin' a long time for fellas to sign a paper!"  Tim groaned as he shoved his hands in his pockets.
"That's cause every decrepit old fart for twenty miles is tryin' to sign up."  George threw disapproving glances at men he though too old for soldering.
"It's a wage I guess and I figure that there's a fair share of boys as bored as we are with country life."  Bethel commented as she stepped further in the line.
It was half an hour later when she crossed the threshold and stood before the table of recruiters. There were two officers and a sergeant named Pleasant Henry. All wore new uniforms unsullied by the blood and mud of future days. The noble gray and polished buttons impressed the young woman and made her heart stir all the more for the adventure waiting her in the 2nd Tennessee army.

"What's your name son?" Sgt. Henry prepared to write; his Irish accent still evident after years in America. His irises were a piercing blue that demanded truth in all communication.

Bethel stood at attention, her eyes meeting the sergeant's. "Tandy Scott, sir."

"Where ya from?"

"Washington County near Longmire."

Henry leaned forward, squinting. "You eighteen?"

"Twenty."

The sergeant let out a breath. "Sure ya are. Sign here or make your mark."

"I can read and write." Bethel retorted.

"Good for you. You are now a soldier in the Confederate States Army. Now assemble outside with the rest of your brethren, Private Scott!"

George grins broadly and slaps his sister on the back "I'll see ya outside, Private Scott." He shouts as she leaves the building.

"Just who are you, Mr. Mouth?" One of the officers inquired as he watched another volunteer sign his name.

"George Erwin, sir."

Sgt. Henry frowned. "You don't look eighteen to me, boy."

George appeared amused to be questioned just after a woman walked right past them. "I am sir! My birthday was two months ago."

"Don't get yer feathers all fluffed out. I'm gonna let ya die for the cause. Where ya from?"

"Washington County"

"Sign here then join the others outside." Henry handed the pencil to George.

He signed his name under Tandy Scott. "That all you need?"

"We'll get more information from ya when we muster in at Lynchburg. Next!"

        The three of them stood around shooting the breeze with recruits from all over the state. Most were farmer's sons, men out of work or young men itching for a diversion from small town or country life. Some even joined to fight for the cause, though the cause was not all that clearly defined. One thing that Bethel figured out early on was that freeing slaves had little to do with volunteering. No one volunteering to fight owned any slaves or knew anyone that did. Most were simply bored or poor.

A heavy set man with sergeant stripes emerged from the station and began shouting as he grabbed confused recruits. Bethel was one of the four he snatched and placed an arm's length apart.

"The rest of ya fall behind these fellas and be quick about it. Equal numbers in each line, now move!"

Tim and George rush in behind Bethel. There were a total of one hundred soldiers in the newly formed "A" company. Sgt. Moore stood before them, legs spread wide and hands behind his back. His paunch reminded Bethel of Santa Claus.

"You gentlemen are no longer human beings, but members of company A and A stands for arseholes. You will listen to every word I say and learn the first time. I am standing at parade rest and now I will stand at attention. I am going to pivot around and this command is called, about face!"

Moore spun around with his back to the troops. "Company, forward, march! For those of ya too stupid to figure it out, march means walk."

Bethel and George found the man's Irish brogue amusing. They appeared proud and cocky to their timid cousin who was having second thoughts about seeing the elephant for the first time. He shouldn't have listened to those old farts in the dry goods store go on about past military days and the glory that went along with it.

The new soldiers were taken to a field outside of Nashville where they were emersed in the reality of army life. They pitched tents that were crammed full to bursting with scared, excited, naive young men, many of which had not washed in weeks. The grass was all worn away in the field and the rain had created a thick, sucking mud in its wake. After the downpours, it was hot and steamy like the Amazon jungles Bethel had read about. She hardly could see how South America could be any worse.

After three weeks it seemed that they had never been anything except privates in the 2nd Tennessee infantry. They drilled constantly and when not marching back and forth across the muddy fields, the green troops practiced loading and firing muskets. Some were greener than others when it came to firearms.

One such a lad was a tent mate of theirs named Joseph Paul. He was a watch maker's son who had at one time no other ambition outside of taking over the family business, but the call for volunteers had flicked his ear as hard as any school bully. Joe's great grandfather had fought in the War of 1812, regaling the wide-eyed grandchildren with heroic takes of the battlefield, making them all ardently wish for the same opportunity. It was an adventure if one enjoyed mosquitoes, nasty food, bad tempered drill sergeants and the Tennessee two-step.

Bethel liked Joe who was mild mannered and slow to anger, even though camp life pushed everyone to the brink. He was blond haired and thin with long fingers like a pianist. Joe looked every bit like the watchmaker he was, but nothing like a soldier. A thin book of poetry remained always in his right rear pocket. The elegant letters he wrote home to his parents, amazed Bethel and George as they gave such a dignity to their suffering and they made them all believe that they were doing the right thing.

For Bethel and her kin, the running and shooting were nothing new, but Joe Paul and the other city boys had a time of it. Joe knew nothing at all about guns and could not load and shoot fast enough to please Sgt. Moore, who got so angry that he spit the obscenities in Paul's face. That sort of teaching method might work wonders with some people, but was only making poor Joe perform worst.

George and Bethel tried to work with him but in the end Joe was among a dozen or so recruits who were sent home as being unfit for service. Two years later there would be no such reprieve for those unable or unwilling to soldier. Even though the man was humiliated, Bethel was glad to see him get to go home. She didn't think it would have happened otherwise. Three weeks later the 2nd Tennessee was bound for Virginia on a troop train. The mood was light, the air filled with laughing and singing in anticipating the experience ahead.
*********

May 31, 1861 found Bethel, George and Tim hunkered down for the night. Periodically a shot rang out from across Aquia Creek. Soon someone from their side returned fire.

"Goddamn it, we just mustered in and the Yanks are at us already." George mumbled, though secretly excited about the ordeal.

Bethel lay on her stomach with her rifle cradled in her arms, the starry night above reminded her of stretching out on the porch roof at home and wondering what was up there. A bullet whistled through the air. The shots were coming from the trees some hundred yards away. Tim is next to her on his back, his weapon clinched tightly to his chest.

"How did you intend to shoot like that?" Bethel asked, with a hint of smart ass.

"Aw, I'll get a chance soon enough."

The sound of a horse's hooves beating the ground interrupted the conversation. It was Colonel Bates riding the length of the line. He was repeating the same command has he rode along.

"Hold your fire! Don't waste the ammo. We're out of range and they can't see us. Hold your fire!"

The chestnut mare snorted behind George and Bethel, the Colonel took on an unearthly appearance against the dark star pocked sky. He turned the horse and went on down the line shouting his command to save the ammo into the cool night air, frogs and crickets harmonizing like backup singers.

"It's weird ain't it?" George asked.

Bethel gave him a puzzled look in response.

"This is just like back home when we used to camp out and fish all night. Don't seem like it should still be the same, us being soldiers and all." He let out a belch.

Bethel nudged him. "Yeah, things shouldn't seem this normal!"

The chattering of teeth make them both look at Tim. "I got chilled; it's cold along this creek. Aw, what's it matter? We'll be back home in a few weeks anyways. "

Their first taste of war was slight as was the next nibble at Bull Run that July, 1861 near Manassas, Virginia where the 2nd Tennessee was positioned at Union Mills ford on Bull Run creek. George, Bethel and Tim are about one quarter mile from a railroad bridge over the creek being defended by General Ewell's brigade, much to their disappointment as the three of them were becoming antsy for some action.

"I thought we see the elephant by now." Bethel grumbled. She had no idea of why combat experience was referred to as viewing some animal from Africa, but everybody used it.

"George scowled as watched the bridge in the distance. They were to support the troops guarding the bridge if needed. "The war will be over by the time we get to do any fighting. Them big mouths back home were probably right when they said it would all be over in a few weeks."

"That will be fine by me! Hear all that ruckus up north there? People are getting' killed!"   Tim pointed to the smoke rising above the trees a short way up the creek with the sound of rifle and cannon fire close enough to promise a stampede of elephants.

George squinted at his cousin. "I never took you for no sissy, what's the matter with ya?"

Tim shoved George. "I ain't no sissy. I want live is all and I don't get the feelin' that's gonna happen."

Bethel had been studying the landscape and finally commented on the situation. "Well, maybe some of them Yanks will avoid the turnpike and try to sneak through this way."

"I sure as shit hope so. All we do is drill and wait and drill and wait!"

Another private, Tom Dalton, lay his musket down and pulled a pipe from his breast pocket. Their uniforms were not gray, but a butternut color and not that well made. The shoes or boots they wore were whatever they had showed up with when they signed the paper to join up, as well as the undershirts, which gave the regiment a colorful appearance.

 Tom lit his pipe, pulled in some tobacco fumes and blew smoke toward the Warrenton Turnpike. "I hear ya, all the fun is over yonder."

"Sounds like all hell is breakin' loose and we're missing every goddamned bit of it, son-of-a-bitch."   George seemed almost ready to pout.

"If we lose that railway, we're in trouble that's why. The Yanks would love to stop our supply route."   Bethel had to admit that she wanted to be in the fight too. Being on the outside of things was not an Erwin tradition.

Tim let out a sigh. "It'll suit me just fine if this whole mess is over by Thanksgiving."

Tom and Bethel both watched the battle in the distance, expressions of doubt etching their features. Those thinking that the "fun" would be over in a few weeks were many; memories of past wars had dulled in the public conscious. Tom was older than the three young soldiers at age thirty and placed a hand on Tim's shoulder.

"I hope so, son. Let's all hope so."

"Well, if don't end soon I don't want to spend the whole war watching everybody else do the soldiering." George aimed his rifle north toward the battle. The sound of cannon balls pounding the earth and the thick black smoke hovering in the distance scared all of them down deep.

## Chapter Seven
Several Months Later


After supper Jane Erwin opened a letter from Bethel to read to the family at the dining room table. Her parents were not happy with the stunt she and her brother pulled and planned a good thrashing when they returned home, but what was done was done. Now they prayed daily that the three of them would make it through the war unscathed. So far the mail service ran well enough that this was the fourth letter since joining up in Nashville. Everyone was anxious to get started so Jane put on her reading glasses and began reading.

"This one is from Huntsville. She says they captured two Federal ships full of supplies in Virginia and they reenlisted for three years or the rest of the war, whichever comes first."

Joy shook her head. "I just can't believe she's doing actually doing it. Nobody notices she ain't a man?"

"No surprise really. Bethel can do whatever she has a mind to." Mildred smiled slightly.

Ed Erwin had a wild look in his young eyes. "I can't wait for my turn!"

His father slapped his hand on the table. "This family has given more than enough to this damned war already."

Jane peered over glasses at her husband. "Anyone care to hear the rest?" Bill nodded his head and sat back in the chair. "They're on their way to Corinth, Mississippi. She says that there's two brothers in their company that have a colored boy along to cook for them and he's a lot better than them army cooks!" She chuckled. "That's what I'm talking about! This is a rich man's war and they got poor fools to play in it." Bill seemed justified.

"Well now, three of them fools is ours and we got to take what comes." Mildred chastised her son who scowled and folded his arms. "How is she fooling everbody? What does she say about going to the, you know?" Joy asked, not really fathoming her sister's charade. "She hasn't said a word about having any trouble, but George and Tim are bashful about private things too, so I don't imagine that Bethel is all that different." Jane held the letter as if it were the last one.

Mildred reached over and took Jane's hand. "Maybe this foolishness will be over soon. So far, they've managed to escape injury. Lord let it all send soon."

* * * * * * **

In November the war still raged on with no sign of finishing. It had also come closer to home with nearby railroad bridges being torched by union loyalists to cut supply lines to the east.

Bill Erwin was repairing fence on the hill pasture overlooking his house when he heard men on horse back yelling. They were Confederate soldiers searching for the unionists who had burned the bridges a few days earlier. An officer dismounted and approached the house.

Jane watched from the screen door the man walked up to the house leading his horse. He had five men with him in fine, new gray uniforms courtesy of their rich benefactor who waited back by the barn.

"My name is Lt. Stanton. Where is your husband, Mrs. Erwin?" Louis Stanton was tall and thin with a handle bar mustache. His father was a druggist in Johnson Station and prior to the military he was a pharmacy student.

"What do want with Bill? He's working in the north pasture." Jane placed her hands into her apron pockets trying not to appear nervous. Stanton reached into his saddlebag and threw a piece of burnt wood on the ground. He remained silent while watching her reaction. It was common knowledge that many of the families in the area harbored Union sympathies.

"He had nothing to do with that! Bill, Bill!" Jane shouted to her husband as he ran past the mounted soldiers.

"Just what the hell do you want?" Bill stepped onto his porch in a defensive stance.

"How have you been spending your nights lately, Bill? The officer pushed the charred wood toward the porch steps.

"I got kin wearing that damned uniform. I didn't burn any bridges and don't appreciate the accusation." Bill's mouth turned down into a deep frown, his Adam's apple bouncing up and down as if to stifle more abusive language.

"Ain't no secret how you all feel about the Union. Where were you two nights ago?" Stanton took two steps toward the shorter man, but was cautious of the claw hammer in his hand.

"Sittin' by the fireplace where I am every damned night after I've worked my ass off. " The soldiers mumbled among themselves prompting Bill to point a finger at them. "I know all you fellas. Jimmy, we looked after you as a child when your mother fell ill. You all got some nerve coming to my place with guns and threatening me!"

The barn door creaked open as Ed emerges leading Cathy in tow. He held a shot gun in the crook of arm. The mounted soldiers turn suddenly in alarm as the boy points the gun at them. One pulls a pistol.

"You ain't gonna hurt my Pa!" Ed screams in his most menacing voice.

Jane ran off then porch, slipping out of Bill's grip. They both ran to their son until Stanton told them to stop.

"Ed, drop the gun boy. These soldiers were just leaving. They just asked me a question is all." Bill gestured to the ground.

Stanton motioned for the men to put their weapons down. "Put the gun down, son. Put it down. We're not gonna hurt your Pa."

The cow, anxious to move onto the pasture, bumped into Ed. The shotgun fired hitting one of the soldier's horses and the rider shot the boy in panic. The child was blown backwards onto his back, blood dying his shirt bright red.

Jane let out a mournful cry, shaking Bill out of a momentary stupor. He grabbed Ed's gun and pointed it Stanton as his son's head rolled to the side, blood pouring from his mouth. "You no good sons of bitches better get the hell out outta here! I wish had burned them goddamned bridges!"

"We got two kids fightin' for your damned cause and this is how the Confederacy repays us?" Jane cradled Ed's head in her lap, his vacant eyes staring up at heaven.

Mildred Carter appeared behind the soldiers on the crest of the hill, squirrel gun in hand like some avenging angel. "Don't none of ya ever again ask for my help and that goes for all future generations of yer kin. Now git on outta here before I send some of ya to the devil a few years early."

The soldiers look ashamed at the death of the boy and lack the bravado and sense of purpose they had when riding up minutes before. Mildred motioned with the gun barrel for them to depart, her face a mask of disgust and hatred. As Stanton turned his horse around he looked back at Bill Erwin.

"You heard the woman and you won't be told again."

Grandma Carter went to the lifeless boy and pulled his shirt back. "His poor little heart is shredded. Jesus will look after him now."

\*\*\*\*\*\*\*\*\*\*\*\*\*\*\*\*\*\*\*\*

The dark sky rumbled its discontent and drenched the Virginia countryside with a heavy, cold rain. Bethel and George huddled in a dog tent reading the letter from home. The small tent was pocked with holes and they shielded the paper between them with their hands. George pounded the earth with his fist and Bethel shook her head with a quivering lip. He sees his sister begin to cry and gives in too.

"Killed by our own people and he was just a little boy." He wiped his face with a dirty sleeve.

"I'm not sure which side we're really on anymore when our families aren't safe at home. We eat maggots, wear rags, and sleep in the mud, just so our own army can shit on our folks! Damn it hell!" Bethel's voice was laced with anger.

"I feel like I should be home protecting them, but I thought that's why we joined the army."

George nodded his head. "Me too."

# Chapter Eight
Corinth, Mississippi
May 1862

Anna Harold roamed around Cohen's Grocery filling a small basket with fruit, flour and lard for an apple pie. The floor boards creaked under her thin frame bearing a dark blue dress with tiny pink flowers. The next day was her daughter's birthday and though pies were an extravagance with the war on, Anna wanted to make the day special. She took the basket up to the counter where Carl Cohen waited, smiling brightly.

"Mr. Cohen, you are one of the very few honest men around here who has not raised his prices. I do thank you for that."

Cohen, balding and just over fifty with a stocky build, winked.

"Well, Anna, I think that bad times are coming and I'd like to score a few points with Him!" He pointed at the ceiling.

"I'd like to pay my bill in full this time." Anna never liked to use credit and only did so when the work slowed down, which had not been a problem since the troops had moved into the area.

"You're doing well with washing the troop's laundry? We do what we can for our families and maybe one day we will meet in heaven some day." Cohen smiled warmly at the young woman at his counter.

"Between you and me, I do it more for the money. Ain't easy raising a little one alone." Anna pulled a CSA five dollar note from her purse. "I'd like the change added to my account for a rainy day."

"You're a smart lady, Anna. I too always like to have a little something to fall back on in case one day the cart has no horse!" He opened a large ledger and inscribed the deposit under the Harold name.

"Thank you, Mr. Cohen. I know it isn't easy staying in business now." She looked around the sparsely stocked store.

"Me and my wife will keep going as long as we can. You must come by this Friday and join us for our Sabbath meal. Mrs. Cohen loves having little Ella around. You know, we've not been blessed with grandchildren yet!" He chuckled.

"I'd like that Mr. Cohen. We'll see you then."

Anna stepped out onto the wooden sidewalk then strolled down the cobblestone street. The wind gently tossed her hair and she smiled at the hustle and bustle in the city. At times one could almost imagine that there was no war, if it weren't for the scum that took advantage of the situation.

A group of men standing across the street in front of a hardware store watch as Anna walks down the street, her pretty skirt swaying with each step. They laugh and whisper among themselves until one of them wanders over to her.

Kyle Sims removed his hat. "Good day to, Mam. How are you this morning?"

Anna had noticed the men off to her left and knew they were up to trouble. She studied the unshaven man for a second whose greasy hair lay plastered to his forehead.   "I'm quite fine, thank you." She continued to walk, but more briskly.

Sims kept up with her. "Could I buy you a cup of coffee? My name's Kyle, Kyle Sims."

"While I appreciate such a kind offer, Mr. Sims, I really need to get home and finish up the chores."

Sims glanced back at his friends who snickered at his lack of success. "Where might that be? I could sure help a gentle lady like yerself around the place."

Anna turned to him. "Woman's chores sir, just woman's work."

He grabbed her arm. "I'm just trying to help you, a woman all alone."

"My status in life is no concern of yours!"  Anna was alarmed that he knew she was a widow. "I don't appreciate your attitude, Mr. Sims."

Sims' pals hooted and hollered at her response. "You're too good for me, is that it?"

"Not at all, Mr. Sims." Anna knew that he was in a bad situation, as was she, and hoped they could both get out of it without consequences. "I simply do not have time for socializing today."

"Watchca got there, a picnic basket? You goin' on a picnic with yer fella?" He snatched the basket from Anna.

"Give that back! I have a child to feed." She could no longer keep the anger from her eyes and hoped that it hid the fear that also lurked in them.

"Not till you treat me like a gentleman." Sims growled.

Anna's pale cheeks flushed with indignity. "I'm afraid that you shall not live that long!" At that moment Anna looked into the gray eyes of a handsome bearded young man. Bethel and George Erwin stood behind Sims.

"Give it back to her." Bethel stated, smoothly.

Sims turned around and then grinned. "Oh shit, it's two soldier boys. I am so scared."

Bethel grabbed the basket from Sims and handed it to Anna.

George looked disgusted. "Ought to be ashamed of yerself for pickin' on a lady."

"Why don't you mind yer own business?" Sims moved close to George who was somewhat shorter.

"Why don't you go find a whorehouse since that's more suitin' to yer personality." Bethel hissed into Kyle's ear.

Sims' gang approached and Anna feared for her two rescuers, "I'll just be on my way, gentlemen. There's no need for trouble."

Bethel removed her hat and bowed gracefully, prompting George to laugh as his showboating sister. Sims bent down, grabbed a handful of horse manure and threw it at George, who ducked sending the foul smelling debris all over Anna. Bethel threw Sims a mean look then drew her fist back. As Sims prepared to be slugged, she kicked him the nuts. "The rest of us want some too? I got enough to go around!"

George moved into a boxing stance.

"Come on, let's go!" Bethel stated with a warning tone.

Sims' gang tried to help him up as he rolled around holding his crotch. A red faced Kyle croaked out obscenity laced instructions to let them go as the two soldiers escorted Anna through down the street.

Bethel and George walked with Anna Harold down the main street to the out skirts of Corinth where she stopped before a small farm. The Harold house was a two-story L-shaped wood structure with a wraparound porch. The paint was beginning to show wear from the weather and lack of maintenance. She offered the soldiers lemonade and asked them if they could sit for a spell.

The two siblings sat on the porch swing together while Anna sipped her drink in a wicker chair. She was pretty and graceful with a back drop of yellow roses that entwined through a trestle on the porch rail. "I thank you boys much for the help. I've seen you both in camp." Anna smiled sweetly as she watched the slice of lemon sink in her glass. She saw the confused look on Bethel's face. "I do the laundry for many of the men and sometimes help with nursing. I keep a tent on the camp grounds to work. What are your names?"

"Well, I'm Tandy Scott and this George Erwin. Afraid we don't have extra money to have our laundry done or we'd sure help ya out some."

George giggled as he swung gently in the swing. "No kiddin' ya there. I'm not much good at washin' clothes as ya can see!"

"Tell ya what, you bring your clothes by and I'll clean them up for ya. I owe ya both that much." Anna winked at Bethel who cocked her head like a puzzled dog.

George sat up straight. "You don't owe us nothin' Mam. He had it coming to him."

Anna cleared her throat and sat the glass on a small table next to her chair. "Please call me Anna. Mam makes me sound like your grandmother! Come by and we can visit while I wash your clothes."

"We really would appreciate that, Anna. I think my uniform is more dust than cloth." Bethel was irritated at George's interest in their new friend, but she was not sure why. She really didn't understand her desire for Anna's attention either.

George pulled the lemon from his glass and sucked on it. "Who was that fella botherin' you?"

Anna let out a sigh. "Kyle Sims. His daddy owns a large plantation with around a hundred slaves, so the Sims are exempt from fighting."

Bethel nodded her head thinking of the many dinner table conversations with their father. "The sentiment back home is that this is a rich man's war and the poor get to fight it."

"My husband agreed, but wouldn't have found for the Union because he felt very strongly about the state's rights to govern them…I just think it's all just an excuse to preserve the southern way of life." Anna's tone lowered.

"Where is he now?" Bethel asked gently.

"I'm a widow. Michael died last winter of pneumonia."

Her two guests both looked down at their scruffy boots. "Sorry, we don't mean to pry." George mumbled.

Anna turned toward them and placed her hands on her knees. "You didn't mean anything by it. Would you boys like to stay for supper?" Me, Billie Jean and Ella would enjoy the company. Billie Jean is my sister and Ella is my little girl."

Before they could answer Anna stood up. "If you boys could catch a chicken and wring its neck for me and chop some wood we'll have us a nice dinner. Bring it all through the back door when you're done. I'll get started with the baking. Oh, and go down into the cellar in the barn and fetch a jar of apple butter."

"Chickens are your specialty; I'll get the apple butter!" George laughed and hopped off the porch.

Bethel's lips slipped into a crooked grin. "That's who I trust with my life."

George emerged from the barn with a jar of apple butter as his sister surveyed the yard for the right chicken. She spotted a fat white one and chased after it while her brother placed the jar on the back porch steps. He laughed hysterically as Bethel dived for the bird and hit the dirt, feathers flying.

"Shit, damn it hell!" Bethel cursed as her chin bounced off the ground.

"It helps to be smarter than the chicken ya know?" George ducked as his sister picked up a dirt clod and threw it at him.

She rose to her knees and waited for the bird to settle down. George walked around to block the chicken from heading further away. When it came back toward Bethel she grabbed it, causing it to cackle and squirm in her arms. She could see Anna watching them from the kitchen window and suddenly felt foolish, so when she stood up Bethel bowed gracefully toward the window then turned away and rung its neck.

George caught the carcass after Bethel tossed it to him and it placed on a stump where an axe was buried in the wood. He pulled it out and chopped the bird's head off.

"I can't believe we get to eat real food. I don't know if my gut will know what to do with it."

Bethel seemed far away for a moment then responded, "It has been a long time hasn't it? Who could have guessed that a home cooked meal would ever be a luxury?"

Inside the house the two sisters watch the young soldiers goofing off. Anna smiles and her eighteen year old sister, Billie Jean, studies her face then shrugs.

"Who are they?" Billie Jean asks, her brown hair hanging loose from a morning bath.

"A couple of Union boys who came to my rescue in town." Anna reached into a wooden bin and pulled out several large potatoes and took them to the table. "Would you bring me a knife and a bowl?"

Still watching the soldiers in the yard Billie Jean retrieved a large white bowl from the cupboard. "We do have more riff raff running around these days."

Anna took the bowl from her sister and gestured at the stove. Billie Jean placed several half logs in the stove belly. "Well, this trash was local. Horace Sim's brat. I've heard him harass the ladies before and it must have been my turn today."

Billie Jean stoked the fire then brought another knife to the table. "I noticed that Kyle isn't wearing a uniform. Would it not be a fair thing to have money?"

"Not just money dear, slaves. Owning slaves is the ticket out of the war."

Billie Jean looked out the window. "And fine young men like that have to pay for their crimes."

Anna grinned and kept peeling potatoes. "Yes, it is a shame. Which one causes you the most anguish?"

"The one chopping wood. His time could be so much better spent than hanging around some old army camp!"

Later that early evening the four new acquaintances sit in the living room together. George and Bethel sit at opposite ends of a lush green sofa. The two sisters sit in parlor chairs with a small, round table between them sipping lemonade.

"You two looked like you're related." Billie Jean stated.

Bethel, caught off guard, clears her throat. "We're first cousins."

"Tell me, what is life like in the Tennessee Mountains?" Anna smiled sweetly, almost maternally.

"Hard, just plain hard. Most everybody is a farmer, but there are some shop owners and blacksmiths, one doctor, that kind of thing. Both our fathers farm." George missed home, but really did not miss the backbreaking labor.

Bethel leaned forward, resting her glass on one knee. "What did your husband do, Anna? If you don't mind me asking?"

"He was a lawyer. Mike had many wealthy clients, including slave owners, but many times he worked for free or took food and other goods as payment. That's why my cellar is still so full." She shook her head. "He was too kind at times."

George looked puzzled. "He worked for nothing?

"Yes, if someone could not pay he did not turn them down. Anyone might need help, but not everyone has money. Mike took what they could afford to give."

Anna seemed to sadden so Bethel chimed in. "I'd like to study medicine, you know, at a real school. My granny is a healer and I help the surgeon with the sick and wounded at camp."

"Yeah, a lot of the men go to Tandy instead of old Bonebreak, that's what we call Captain Marsh the surgeon. He does stupid things like give ya salts for the trots or let pus form on a bullet wound. Tandy is real smart when it comes to healin'. George beamed and elbowed his sister.

Anna smiled warmly at Bethel who blushed. "Well, it's good to have a friend who can cure your ails."

"Oh, I'm not that clever. Grandma Carter is the smart one. She taught me everything I know." Bethel found herself watching the soft light glide through the window and paint highlights in Anna's hair.

Billie Jean suddenly stood up. "It sure is stuffy in here. Think I'll go sit on the porch for a spell. Smells like it could rain." She rolled her eyes in George's direction.

He nodded his head. "Maybe I should have a look at them clouds. We don't want to get caught in a storm."

Bethel's lips slipped into a crooked grin. "No, we wouldn't want that at all."

George winked at Bethel then followed Billie Jean outside, slipping his cap back on as he went through the front door. The screen door banged shut behind the two teenagers with both choosing the porch swing.

Anna shook her head remembering the first pangs of love years ago. How had so much time passed?

Bethel peered over at the dishes still on the table and the pots near the sink. "Why don't I give ya a hand with those dishes?"

Somewhat surprised, Anna replied, "Oh, you're my guest. I wouldn't ask you to do that."

Bethel stood up and offered her hand to Anna. "It's my pleasure. It's been a long time since we had a decent meal and good company. I do get tired of being surrounded by dirty soldiers day in and day out. "

Anna took Bethel's hand and gracefully rises from the chair with a knowing glint in her eye that the young soldier misses. "You know, kind sir, there are a fair number of people that would think it improper for us to be alone in the house or for them to be without a chaperone on a porch swing."

Glancing out the screen door at George and Billie Jean, Bethel began to gather silverware from the table. She responds with a hint of sadness. "Well, I've seen a lot of things in the past months that was a long way from proper. Us washing dishes together is nothing at all anymore."

"I quite agree, but it is a tragedy that such a nice young man should be spending his days at war instead of discovering the joys of youth." Anna put a large pot on the stove to heat water.

Bethel chuckled. "You make me sound so noble." She became nervous as Anna stood beside her. What was going on with her? Bethel's heart pounded as the sweet smelling woman smiled and chatted with her.

"We'll let the water come to a boil then add some cold water from the pump. We never had many luxuries, but Mike did insist that we have an indoor water supply. I add just enough cold water that I can stand it."

"I've washed dishes before, Anna." Bethel replied, amused at the instruction.

Anna studied her guest for a moment. "Well, then you'll make some lucky woman a fine husband, Tandy. My late husband never washed a dish in his life. His mother washed his dishes and clothes, and then I took over."

Bethel bit her lip in thought. "I understand more than you know. Granny wants me to take over as a healer, but I don't want to live my while life in those hills. Particularly now that I've been a few places."

Anna Harold peered outside at a roll of thunder in the distance. "As much as we enjoy your company, you and George best be heading back. It's liable to start pouring any minute."

"I don't mind getting wet. I was born on a rainy night and I've loved rain ever since. But you're right. If we're late we'll really catch the devil for it. We'll do the vigett all night long!"

Anna followed Bethel into the living room to the front door. "You would make a wonderful doctor, Tandy Scott. You take care that you make it through this damned war."

"I worry some about you two being on your own out here." Bethel felt reluctant to leave after remembering the reason they became acquainted with the sisters.

"We'll be fine." Anna kissed the young soldier on the cheek. "You are welcome here any time." Billie Jean leaned forward in the porch swing to stare at Anna. "You and your cousin are welcome any time." She added, which seemed to appease her sister.

Bethel was speechless after the warm kiss and felt a tingling in her chest and loins. She smiled broadly, retrieved her cap from the oak tree near the door and placed it on her head. There was a crack of thunder that released a torrent of rain. George let out a yelp.

"I bid you fair well, Madame." Bethel opened the screen door and caught a nose full of rain scented air. She grabbed George's arm, pulling him off the swing and the two ran down the steps through the yard to the dirt road, laughing and carrying on like school boys.

**Chapter Nine**
Corinth Road
April 5, 1862

Shots rang out through the dense fog where the Confederate troops looked like ghosts as they struggled in the sucking mud. The heavily traveled road was liquid dirt after days of heavy rain. Someone ahead of Bethel slips and is caught by the men on both sides of him. She frowns deeply and pulls her kepi further down over her face to ward off the chilling rain.  Tim shivers to her left and George sneezes to her left.

It is unlikely that the sniper can see anything well enough to hit it, but the shots remind everyone there are more worries that day than being frozen, tired and hungry.  She was almost glad that the Yanks fired shots into the blanket of fog or else it would be too easy to day dream about a warm fire at home or sitting at Anna Harold's kitchen table with a hot cup of coffee.   It was too dangerous to get lost in your own thoughts.

The rain came down in sheets with the wind slamming water onto their backs like a neighborhood bully was shoving them down the road.  Shouted orders to march into the field up ahead were passed down through the ranks. They would later learn it was called Fraley Field.

That night the troops camped in the field beneath Shiloh Methodist church which was built of logs and perched on a hill, much like a foreboding angel of death thought Bethel. She and George huddled together under an oil skin blanket with their backs against an old tree. There were few tents with most going to officers and sergeants.

Nearby Tim and another soldier, Dave Bohannon, lie close together on one oil skin and cover up with another. Spooning was really the only way to keep warm in the field while the troops were moving. The rain still fell and the fog eerily rolled across the field.

"I think we're gonna see a herd of elephants tomorrow. I got a real bad feeling this time." George had a cold and shivered in the chilly air.

Bethel listened to the sound of the Union army in the distance. "Me too, it sounds like there's a huge bunch of them Blue Bellies waiting for us. I'm glad we got our letters wrote yesterday." George smelled the wet pine trees and wished like hell he was back home on a camping trip. "You afraid to die?"

"I don't know. I ain't been that scared so far, but we haven't been in nothing like the fightin' in Virginia. I'm more afraid for Ma and Pa after what happened to Ed. Damn." Bethel wanted the night to quit dragging. The waiting was worse than the fighting.

"I was ready to die for the cause, whatever that might be, but since meetin' that Billie Jean…."

Bethel snickered.

"What? I wouldn't laugh. I think her sister likes you and I mean REALLY likes you!" George's eyes grew wide.

"No, no, can't be. Wish we had some pop skull to take the chill off." Bethel tried to change the subject.

Tim suddenly rolled over and handed a bottle to Bethel.

"Where the hell did you get that?" She asked in wonder.

Tim grunted. "Took it off that son-of-a-bitch sutler yesterday. Goddamned thief!"

Bethel took a swig then handed the bottle to George who made a face after swallowing it. "Shit, lame crap. Must be Yankee whiskey cause nobody from the hills would waste a good glass bottle on it."

"Damn right, glad I didn't pay fer it. He had a bunch of them bottles with different labels on them. Sure it was all the same shit though." Tim reached for the bottle and George give it back reluctantly.

"I saw one of them peddlers get the hell beat out of him in Virginia. Deserved it too with the prices he was chargin'." A clap of thunder sent a downpour that made the soldiers pull the oil skins back over their heads.

Tim shouted, "Why did we sign up again?"

\*\*\*\*\*\*\*\*\*\*\*\*\*\*\*\*\*\*\*\*

That morning around ten o'clock the 2nd Tennessee was dodging bullets in a thick grove of trees near an abandoned farm road that in history books would be called, The Hornets' Nest. It was very hot and humid and the bullets whizzing by sounded all the world like a hoard of angry wasps. Clouds still hung in the sky. George and Bethel stay close as they struggle with the rest of the Confederate army to keep the blue coats at bay. They have not seen Tim for some time. George suddenly drops into a thicket of brush and Bethel kneels beside him.

"Are you hit?" She yelled.

George shakes his head and covers with ears with his hands. "It's the Goddamned noise! I got a headache from Hell! I can't think straight."

She reached into the mud and rolls it into a ball. "Here, try it."

George looked at the mud ball in her hand then shrugs and sticks it in his right ear. "Not bad, try it!" He rolls another mud ball for the other ear.

Bethel shoves mud into her ears as a Minnie ball whizzes by making her duck to the left. "Let's keep moving."

As they follow their colors a private from the 1st Tennessee is hit by a cannon ball. It tears the man's leg off. He screams and falls to the ground. The leaves and brush on the ground have dried out in the intense heat and the bullets hitting the earth ignite small fires all around the wounded. A bullet lands near the fallen private starting a fire that spreads to his sleeve. The terrified man screams and attempts to get up.

Bethel hollered at George to grab his arm while she grabbed the good leg. They pulled him behind a shade tree for some cover then she beat out the fire with her cap. The mangled leg bled profusely as he begged for water. George poured water from his canteen into the private's mouth.

As blood gushed from the wound Bethel asked the man if he was wearing a belt. He groans and shakes his head.

George put a finger under the private's red suspenders. "This work?"

"Yeah, cut me a piece off."

Using a rusted pocket knife George cut a long strip and handed it to his sister who wrapped it tight and tied around the upper thigh.

"What are ya doin'?" The private lifted his head.

"Stoppin' the bleed', you might make it home this way." Bethel patted his shoulder.

"I never did hear of such a thing."

George smiled. "The surgeon's got better gadgets, you'll see soon enough."

"I wish I could do more for ya, but try to hold on until somebody can move ya. It might be some time yet." Bethel tried to comfort the young man whose hands shook from the pain and shock. Tears rolled down his cheeks. The noise around them was deafening and a thick, blue acrid smoke hung in the air.

Tim appeared, shouting, "Come on! We're crossing the field."

Bethel squeezed the wounded man's hand and gave him a nod. She did not feel right leaving him but had no choice.

\*\*\*\*\*\*\*\*\*\*\*\*\*\*\*\*\*\*\*\*\*\*

The Yanks had set up camp in several log cabins on the edge of Ross field and were caught unaware. The Rebs attacked and killed many horses and damaged artillery before the Union troops could gain control.

Confederate Colonel J. Know Walker rode the line of infantry at the edge of the forest. Before him lay Ross field which was some three hundred yards. He watched as the 1st and 9th Tennessee Infantries charged ahead with his sword raised. The Yanks waited until the last group was nearly across the field then opened up with artillery and rifle fire from the trees to the north.

The air is tense as George, Bethel and Tim watch the men from the 9th TN Infantry fall. This could be the day they all die. When Walker drops his sword they must take their turn in the taking of the field.

"Double quick time, charge!" Walker shouted and dropped the sword like a guillotine blade.

The 2nd TN charged onto the field and when half way across the Union opened fire from the west at the Hornet's Nest Road where they were protected by a thicket and a fence. The three of them hit the ground as the Yanks open fire. Cannon balls and bullets fill the air above them. The air is hard to breathe or see through because of the dense blue smoke. Bethel looked toward to the nearby pond and saw the wounded crawling to its banks for a drink. The water was tinted red from blood.

"Jesus, did ya ever see such a thing?" She swallowed hard.

"God I wish this day was over." George cringed at the chunks of metal flying overhead.

Tim gawked at the bloody pond and nearly vomited. "That could be us at any minute."

Bethel studied his face and something was different about Tim. "Let's keep moving." She slapped her cousin on the arm. Just follow us and keep down."

"No shit, like I can't figure that out!"

They begin to move, crouching as they walked. A soldier running away knocked George back down prompting him to pronounce the man a chickenshit and a coward. He scrambled quickly back to his feet while Tim fired a shot into the smoke when a Minnie ball buzzed past his ear.

A fellow Confederate emerged from the blue haze and shot Tim in the leg. George grabbed the man's rifle and hit him with it. "Dumb ass!"

The man fell to knees and began sobbing."Stop it, stop it, stop it!!"

"For Christ's sake, we're fighting each other!" Bethel's voiced filled with frustration and anger. "Come on; let's find the rest of the boys. Tim, can you walk?"

Tim winced at the hole in his thigh. "He just grazed me, good thing the bastard couldn't see."

As grape shot tore up the ground around them George grabbed his cousin and sister. "Let's get the hell outta here!"

\*\*\*\*\*\*\*\*\*\*\*\*\*\*\*\*\*\*\*\*

That night in the peach orchard Bethel walked the picket line near the large pond that was already nicknamed, Bloody Pond. It stormed with a vengeance as Union troops fired a shot every so often and the Confederates returned the favor. Heavy rain beat the landscape without mercy.

The air was still filled with acrid smoke and the moaning of the wounded. Sharp flashes of lightening spotlighted pigs feeding on the dead laying in the water. Bethel could not stop the tears from falling down her face and she wondered when the nightmare would end. It felt like the end of the world as she stood vigil in the dark. She tried to recall why she wanted out of those hills so badly. How lucky she would be to living a boring, and mundane life. Simple pleasures now seemed far in the past, like the sunlight coming through the window onto Anna's thin fingers on her coffee cup or listening to Granny Carter chaste somebody for not following orders. What would Bethel would give for a moment of yesterday?

\*\*\*\*\*\*\*\*\*\*\*\*\*\*\*\*\*\*\*\*\*

Early on the morning of April 7, one hundred men of the 2nd TN infantry joined up with the 154th, the 6th and parts of the 15th and 9th TN regiments as they advanced rapidly down the road to the first encampment of the Union army near Shiloh church.

The fighting was intense with General Breckinridge to the east and Major General Polk to the North West.

Major General B.F. Cheatham rode up to Breckinridge who was surveying the battle through field glasses. "I've brought the 2nd Division along, where do you need us?"

Breckinridge lowered the binoculars. "It's bad, but we could hold it if you could cover our left flank to south west of Shiloh church. We are outnumbered, but doing very well."

Cheatham nodded. "I've been very pleased with the performance of my men. They fight with such heart and passion. We'll protect your left flank and hold the line. I'd like to keep the Union from crossing the Shiloh branch if at all possible. They are getting too far south for comfort."

"I couldn't agree with you more!" Breckinridge replied nodding his head as he studied the troop movements below them.

Cheatham turned his horse and galloped on the return trip to his troops.

# Chapter Ten
Shiloh

The fighting was just north of the Shiloh branch of the Tennessee River. The log church was visible high on the hill in the distant northeast. Combat is fierce as each side fires then advances between rounds. German and Irish accents are heard as shouts and curses are hurled. The casualties are high and the field is littered with corpses in bloodied and torn gray, blue and butternut colored uniforms.

Bethel's musket jams and she takes an Enfield rifle off a dead Yank. She also removes his belt and ammo pouch. "Ain't no use in letting a good rifle go to waste." She remarked to George then quickly shot two charging Union soldiers with her newly acquired weapon.

After seeing how much easier the Enfield is to use George scouts around for another one. He spots a bloody Yank still clutching his rifle and tries to pry the man's hands off of it. The wounded Yank struggles to keep the weapon, but blood trickles from the edges of his mouth with the effort and he moans deeply. He asks for water. George looks at Bethel who shrugs and pours water from her canteen into his mouth. He has a hard time swallowing and grabs Bethel's hand.

"I'm scared. It's cold out here. I got a new baby that I haven't……"
The Yank let out a bloody breath and died. George stared at the
clear green eyes that were suddenly lifeless.
"Forget it. Let him keep it. Find another somewheres else." Bethel
lowered her voice in an effort to seem strong.
"I hope all this shit is for a good reason." George remarked, still
glued to the lifeless eyes.

The line of Yanks to the north reloads while Captain Samuel
Vance rides toward the Confederates yelling, "Charge." The Rebs
respond by double quick timing toward the enemy for several
hundred yards. Vance then stops his horse when the troops are just
within range.
Vance raises his sword, "Halt! Ready, aim, fire!"
Bethel is enjoying the Enfield while her brother and cousin must
make do with their ancient muskets. The Yanks fire another round
then charge the Rebels. George doesn't have time to reload before
the blue hoard rushes up, so he screams and runs at them with his
bayonet.

For the next four hours the troops on both sides used every
means necessary to inflict harm on the other side. Swords, fists and
bayonets flew to the tune of cannon fire, pistols and rifles. The
fighting was close and it was hard to tell the soldiers apart in the
confusion and smoke filled air. Bethel was cut with a saber and
George was bashed in the face with the butt of a rifle.
It was hard to even find a place to stand as bodies fell everywhere.
Bethel stumbled several times onto bloody, mangled bodies that only
minutes ago had been either breathing comrades or the enemy. The
ground had given way to spongy, rolling flesh that made it nearly
impossible to find a foothold. The noise made it hard to think or to
reason in any successful way at all.

After what seemed like an eternity, the skirmish ended and
that evening near the river each side gathered their wounded with a
sort of truce in place. The sky was still cloudy and the air humid as
Bethel helped cart the wounded from the battlefield. The mood was
somber and the causalities high. Bethel helped the assistant surgeon,
Bill Chambers, as he went from soldier to soldier assessing wounds.
Her brother and cousin were assigned to place the dead in a line for
identification.

Chambers motioned for Bethel to come close. "All we got is two wheel carts to haul these boys back to camp. Put the ones that have a real chance on the carts. The ones bad off will never survive the ride."

She nodded grimly and returned to aiding the moaning, crying and screaming wounded.

George hollered and waved at the surgeon. "Bill, this one here is still breathin'!" He pointed to one of the men in the dead line.

Chambers, who had been crouching to examine a patient, stood up and wiped his bloody hand on a red stained leather apron. He looked in George's direction. "Tandy, you get some of these fellas onto the carts and I'll go see to this."

"I should get Colonel Bates first; his leg is busted up real bad." Bethel replied.

The soldier given up for dead stared at Bill and George above him. "Son, can you hear me?" Chambers asked.

The private blinked several times. "What happened? Where are we?"

"Looks like a bullet nicked your skull, boy. Battle's all over now." George grinned widely.

The private turned his head to study the man next to him. "That's John Hanna. Is he?"

Chambers turned to George. "Help me get him up. Looks like a Minnie ball grazed his head is all and knocked him out."

George offered a hand to the man on the ground. "We lost alotta boys today. Bill will fix that wound on yer head. Go on with him now. John's in a better place than this now."

\*\*\*\*\*\*\*\*\*\*\*\*\*\*\*\*\*\*\*\*

The next day at the camp outside of Corinth, the surgeons and their assistants worked under open-sided tents performing amputations and suturing wounds. Bethel watched the surgeon, Elmer Hearst, sew a wicked looking gash in a soldier's leg completely closed. Chambers worked on a patient on the next table. The grounds around the tents are covered with recovering patients. Bethel frowns and bites her lip as she studies Hearst's work. "You ought naught sew that clear shut. It'll get morsal just like all the rest of them. The wound needs to drain. You can't let all that fester in there!"

Hearst looked up from his task. The patient is groaning as the surgeon studied Bethel over his spectacles. "That so? You hillbillies come out of those hills thinking you know everything there is to know. Hell, you're not even a dresser, who are you to tell me how to doctor?"

"Private Tandy Scott and I've spent most of my life helping to heal folks."

Chambers turned around, a severed arm in his hand. "Why isn't he a dresser? The men will go to Tandy before any of us, I can guarantee you that."

Hearst mumbles around for a moment. "Well, I don't know. I went to medical school for a year…"

"I didn't! I learned out here in the field first hand." Chambers argued, tossing the limb onto a pile outside the tent. His blood shot eyes bore testimony to a lack of sleep.

Bethel humbled her tone somewhat. "Dr. Hearst, I only want to help and share what I learned from my grandmother. She really is a gifted healer."

Two litter carriers wait for Heart to finish. "Very well, Private Scott, put a dressing on this man and then ship him to Corinth. Anybody that won't heal up in a week send to the hospitals. Bill, train him well, I'm gonna go and see how much progress we've made."

The two litter carriers look to Bethel as Hearst washes his hands off in a bucket of water then rushes out of the tent. She examines the sutures and pulls one out.

"What's yer name, soldier?"

The patient's face displays the strain of fatigue and pain. "Bill Crunk. I am gonna lose that leg?"

Bethel smiled. "No. The last bottom stitch is left open so the wound will drain. Just make sure it gets cleaned with salt water or alcohol. Don't let pus sit in there. You're going on a train ride now, so take care." She nods to the two litter carriers to take him.

Another soldier was brought into the tent screaming and placed on a table before Chambers. "Tandy, come over here and help me."

The patient's eyes widened at the sight of the saw Chambers pulled out of a wooden box. Bill motioned for two soldiers standing nearby to hold the patient's arms. Bethel poured chloroform onto a cloth and placed it over the man's mouth and nose. In the field they did not completely put a patient under, only enough to deaden the pain. The muscles would convulse making it appear to all within sight that the patient was in horrible pain and fighting them off.

The phenomenon did not help the surgeon's already difficult task.

That afternoon George, Tim and several other soldiers dug holes near the tree line to bury the amputated limbs. The blood and decaying flesh was drawing flies as well as dogs and cats, making it nearly impossible to work without insects crawling all over or tumbling over some four-legged beggar. Bethel had cursed a blue moon before Bill finally ordered the trenches dug to stifle the attraction.

It was warm with no breeze, salty sweat rolled down the surgeon's faces stinging their eyes and further made caring for patients draining both physically and mentally. Bethel finished suturing an abdominal wound and had litter carriers take the patient outside. She was exhausted.

"Tandy, in the next tent there's dressings that need changed. After that I think we're done for awhile." Bill looked at his new assistant with blood up to his elbows and on his face where had wiped away the sweat and flies.

"Yes, sir." She went over to a barrel full of water and splashed some on her face then washed the blood and dirt from her arms and hands.

A few yards away stood the tent housing those with bullet wounds that should heal up if infection or dysentery didn't kill the patient first. The shits could be as lethal as any cannon ball in the field.

The young corporal on the cot watched intently as Bethel cleaned the wound and placed a new bandage over it. His attention suddenly went to the front of the tent where Anna Harold stood with a large bag of bandages. He whistles and declares her a sweet sight. Bethel turns around and grins when she sees Anna, who waits outside. The assistant surgeon stands up and walks through the tent toward her. "Hello, what have you brought us?"

"It isn't much, but I made some bandages. I thought you could use them." Anna blushes at the attention she draws from the soldiers. Bethel takes Anna's arm and leads her away from the crowd. "We can use as many as you can find. We haven't had any free time or else me and George would have come by to see if you needed anything, like wood chopped or . . . "

"You have plenty to do here. Billie Jean and I have learned to make do. I'd like to do more than just wash clothes. Do you think I could help care for the wounded?" Anna peers around Bethel at the tent full of patients.

Bill Chambers over heard her and came up behind Bethel. "Yes Mam, these boys can use all the help they can get. Just follow Tandy around and he'll show you what needs done."

Anna smiled sweetly at Bethel who blushed at the hoots and hollers from the men around them. Chambers winked at her then returned to his tent.

"We have a lot of dressings to change, you might be sorry you volunteered." Bethel took the bag from Anna and gestured for her to follow.

"I'm never sorry for good deeds done, Mr. Scott."

## Chapter Eleven

Two Weeks Later
Corinth, Mississippi


Horace Sims puffed on a cigar that he kept tucked into the side of his mouth and draped with a thick, yellowish mustache. He owned a sprawling cotton plantation worked by some one hundred and fifty slaves that did hard labor for only room and board. It was hard for a businessman to make a decent profit when he had to pay wages and Sims had no desire to do so.

Sims sat a round table at one of the best restaurants still remaining in town, The Queen's Pantry, staring out the ornate window onto the street outside. His vest was unbuttoned after an ample steak dinner to allow his equally ample stomach to expand over his lap. The two young men with him were slender and joined him in drinking red wine. One was his son, Kyle Sims.

"Seen much of the war yet, Brandon?" Sims asked the man on his left.

Brandon Neukirk wore a permanent pallor that paired with his blond hair made him always appear ill. The officer's uniform did little to abrade it. "No sir, but I expect to see some action soon. I do wish I had not missed out on Shiloh. Oh, my parents send their best wishes."

"Kyle is itching for some combat experience, but I need him on the plantation when all this fuss is over. Can't risk losing my only heir." Sims coughed and spittle ran down his chin. He removed the cigar and placed it on a pedestal ashtray between himself and Kyle. "I need a strong hand to keep them nigras in line."

Kyle smirked. "That is no lie! They are a difficult breed to control. Can't allow them to hear those uppity nigger lovers from up north putting ideas in their heads neither. We decided I could do my share for the cause in the Provost Guard. It does have its privileges."

Neukirk patted his blond mustache with a burgundy napkin. "My father is quite careful who he allows around his slaves. You are correct about bad influences. Quite frankly, I don't know which is worse, niggers or kikes."

Horace belched loudly. "We have a few of those around here too. Can't trust a word they say and don't even think of turning your back on a Heb. Hell, niggers should own kikes."

Kyle laughed until tears formed and ran down his cheeks. "Oh Dad, that was priceless!" Horace beamed with pride as his son's approval.

Brandon held up his glass in a toast. "To men such as ourselves and the work we must do."

The comrades clinked their glasses together and finished the bottle of wine before stepping outside onto the covered porch.

"What are your plans for the day?" Horace asked Neukirk.

"Well, sir, I have the afternoon off and thought I would see some of the city. I was a child when last here." Brandon sniffed the air then sneezed. "I declare, there is something in the wind here that troubles my nose."

"You sneeze like a girl." Kyle mocked his friend who flashed him a nasty look.

"That's a fine idea, Brandon. Kyle, why don't you show him some of our high lights? I got a little slave trading to do and won't be free for some time." Horace phrased it as a question but his tone was commanding.

"Yes sir, that is one order I don't mind following." Kyle Sims made a deep bow then pulled his friend down the street filled with buggies and wagons.

The two young men smiled broadly and removed their hats as young ladies passed, making Horace suddenly jealous of their youth. He shook it off and walked the short distance to Harper's Slave Auction House.

There was a good crowd and the corners of Sims' mouth turned up when he saw the competition. He should get a good price today. As the auctioneer brought a young boy and girl to the block, a young Negro woman pushed her way through the crowd to Sims. It was his cook; Abby and the children were hers. She was crying and upset, but still in control enough not to touch him or speak too loudly.

"Please, Masta Sims, don't send my children away. They're good workers and strong!" Abby's desperation played on her dark features.

"I know that! I don't need 'em and you got no call telling me how to run my business!" Sims felt a pang of guilt in his chest, but the other gentlemen were watching them. They would gauge his reaction and it could cost him financially.

"Oh sir, I don't mean to be telling you anything at all. I'm just askin' if I could keep my children is all." She hadn't known of the plan to sell the children or Abby would have pleaded her case back on the plantation without an audience.

Horace looked to the two terrified siblings standing high above the crowd. "Abby, it just isn't feasible. I'm sorry, but I can only afford so many mouths to feed. Go on now, get your shopping done and go home." He could see the woman's heart breaking and threw her a bone. "I specified that the children be sold together and I know all these gentlemen here. They won't be far away and I can check on them."

Abby waved and put on a brave face for her two children as the auction began. She knew there was nothing more she could do, but when the bidding started Abby grabbed Horce's arm in desperation and he slapped her hard on the face.

"You do not touch me ever!" Sims was mortified that property of his would actually take such liberties and then stare at him as she now did, eye to eye. She was good though, very good at cooking and managing the household. Abby had learned that from her mother who had died from consumption, which she probably caught from nursing his youngest daughter. Sims did not want to lose her. She would get over losing family members. They all did eventually. It was a fact of life.

"Go on now. Go on home. I expect a wonderful dinner after the hard day I've had!" Sims coughed and cleared his throat, somewhat unnerved at Abby's glare.

*************************

Anna Harold placed spools of multicolored threat and a few yards of material on the counter at White's Sewing Basket. Mildred peered at Anna over small, round spectacles from behind the counter as she laid out her merchandise. The doors to the shop were open to let in what little air moved about and Mildred waved at Mr. Cohn as he swept out his shop across the street. He waved happily at both women.

Someone had tipped over a barrel of peanuts near store entrance and Carl was pushing the nuts onto a dust pan. Anna paid for her purchases, bid Mrs. White farewell then left the store. Two men were in the alleyway between the Cohn store and a hardware store and she recognized one of them as Kyle Sims. She had not seen his companion before. When Carl bent over to pick up the dustpan, Sims kicked the old man in the rear end.

The force of the blow sent Cohn into the bench outside his store. Sims looked to Brandon and giggled. They began to make jokes about Jews. Anna ran over to Carl and helped him up. How could you!" She demanded of the two men.

Kyle smirked. "Well, well, if it ain't the Jew lover. You know, she even married one of them."

Brandon appeared stating and impressive in his uniform. He walked up close to Anna. "Why don't you and your loose sentiments move up north where they prize that sort of depravity? You know, she just might be a spy?"

"What sort of soldier are you? Picking on an old man! If you're so tough why aren't you on the front?" Anna nearly spit on him.

A crowd had started to gather as Anna helped Cohn sit down. Soldiers from Brandon's regiment joined the mob, sneering and shaking their heads at Neukirk and Sims who didn't seem to be nearly as cocky with an audience.

"This is what happens when they let rich scum be the law!" A voice from the crowd declared.

Kyle Sims kicked dirt toward Cohn. He glanced around then pulled on Brandon's sleeve. "Come on, let's get outta here."

Neukirk jerked his elbow away from Sims and stomped toward his men. "Your furloughs are over! Return to camp now!"

The soldiers grumbled and look at him their opinions of Neukirk more than obvious. The crowd began to disperse after Sims and Neukirk shuffle down the street with Sims turning to give Anna an icy glare.

Anna returned the stare then sat next to Carl. "Mr. Cohn, are you alright?"

"Oh Anna, I'm afraid this will cause trouble for you." He shook his head, his features etched with concern.

She smiled. "It will be a sad day indeed when people stand back and watch trash like that harass the honest and innocent."

He removed his glasses and wiped them on his shirt tail that pulled out when he fell. "They already do, my dear. Would you allow me to repay your kindness with a cup of hot tea? Please, you would do me a favor? My wife has a ton of old material that could be used for bandages. Want to see if it is something use can use?"

"Of course, and I'd love some tea." Anna helped the old man up and into his store. When she looked down the street Anna saw that Sims was walking backwards and watching her. Palpitations and a slight hint of nausea told Anna that she should be worried about her act of heroism.

## Chapter Twelve
### Confederate Camp Outside of Corinth


The after math of the latest battle could be seen everywhere in camp. A new grave yard filled up steadily near an embalming tent set up for those who could afford it. Barrels of body parts outside the surgical tents drew a thick fog of flies that buzzed around the limbs and the moaning patients. Bethel appeared drained, bloody and dirty as she stepped away from the tent for break.

Elmer Hearst laid a hand on her shoulder. "Tandy, someday I want to meet that grandmother of your. Cleaning the wounds with salt water, drains in the wounds, it all really works!"

"Well sir, her mother taught her and her mother taught her before that. They had years to figure it out I guess." She smiled weakly.

"You look like shit, boy. Mrs. Harold told me that she has more bandages and lint for us. We'd best get them while we can. Take one of them ambulances into town and fetch them for me. I'll write ya a twenty-four hour pass. Get yerself cleaned up and find something decent to eat, I need you to stay strong. Tomorrow morning you go look for more hospital space and confiscate it." Hearst gave Bethel a little push.

"I have to say I don't ever recall ever being so damned tired, dirty and hungry. Think there's any clean water left in Corinth?"

"I'm sure some of them rich sons-of-bitches have nice wells and they can donate for the cause whether they like it or not." Hearst wiped blood and sweat from his forehead. "Now get on outta here and quit loafing."

Bethel hurried over to the corral where the company horses munched grass after hauling the wounded. She picked a chestnut mare that had not been used in the last round up and hitched her to the closest ambulance. Flies hovering around her face sent Bethel to the water barrel for a quick wash then she hopped up onto the wagon seat and guided the mare down the road to Corinth.

**************************

An hour earlier Anna Harold walked home carrying a basket of material and a beautiful tea cup given to her by Mrs. Cohn. Both sides of the road are thick with trees and brush that gleamed in the sunlight, completely still from the lack of a breeze. It was hot and muggy, almost steamy Anna thought as she made her way the last mile home. She removed her white straw hat to run a hand through her hair.

The sound of hooves brought a sense of relief as perhaps it was a neighbor who could give her a ride the rest of the way. She turned to find Sims and Neukirk on black horses with wild eyes that snorted their discontent. Their hooves stirred up dust as they slowed to a stop.

"Look who have here, Miss High and Mighty." Kyle's voice dripped with menace. He got off the horse, the leather saddle creaking like a rusty door and yanked the hat from Anna's head. Walking around in a prissy manner, Sims mocked her. Neukirk laughed hysterically and dropped to the ground to join his buddy in his parody of womanhood.

Anna Harold fumed. "Give it back. What kind of a boy are you?" Brandon chuckled and led the horses along to keep up with Sims as he pranced around in a circle stirring up dirt and rocks.

"Keep the damned hat!" Anna screamed and walked briskly down the rutted road, holding up her skirt to keep from tripping over it. Sweat ran down her face, mixing with the road dust and it made its way down her cheeks.

Neukirk giggled at Sims who was suddenly embarrassed at being redressed by a woman. Sims chased Anna after Brandon made a clucking sound and flapped his arms. Neukirk mounted his horse and let out a blood curling yell that terrified Anna, spurring her to run faster as he made the stallion prance in a circle.

The woman suddenly sprinted and when several yards ahead of them she turned sharply left into the woods. The brush seemed to part for her as she glided through it, sending a jab of guilt through Kyle. His great grandmother used to say that nature would side with the righteous against evil, like the Red Sea did for Moses. He hesitated.

"Get the bitch! Don't let her get away. Run boy!!" Brandon's eyes glowed with excitement as he dismounted and tied both horses to an old elm tree.

Kyle looked to his friend, a lieutenant in the army. Sims felt inadequate that he could not participate in the war in the only way he considered valid-as a soldier. He plowed through the trees after Anna Harold raging after his own failure. Neukirk followed still whooping and hollering.

Anna was far ahead of the two men as she was familiar with the terrain. She still owned the undeveloped land and had often wandered the forest before the war began. The house was nearly half a mile away where she could lock herself inside with a shotgun. The woods were thick with brush and the ground soggy from days of rain, the tree branches had kept the sun from drying it out completely like the road. Anna darted quickly toward the stream that ran behind her house, tearing her dress on a jagged dead limb. She could hear the men shouting at her, but could not see them.

"We just want to be friends!"

Sims and Neukirk tracked their prey by following trampled leaves and broken limbs. They laugh and giggle like two little boys, calling out to Anna as if she were a playmate. Seeing the flowing creek slows them down as they scour the area for Anna. The only sounds are birds and running water.

Kyle stepped gingerly around a large oak and was smacked full in the face with a thick log wielded by Anna, who took off down the creek bank holding her skirt high. Blood spurted from his shattered nose.

"Shit! Goddamn it, get her now. You've had it down bitch!" Sims screamed with his nose stinging from the blow. Brandon overtook her and knocked Anna to the ground near the stream. He held her while his partner dropped down onto her.

Blood dripped from Sims' nose onto Anna's face as she stared at the man's swollen, misshapen features. His eyes burned with hatred and vengeance as the cold water soaked her back and hair. Neukirk grabbed her hands and spun her around out of the water.

Sims unbuckled his belt and pushed his pants down to reveal a small, erect penis. "It's my turn now you whore." The words hissed from his mouth.

He rammed himself into her over and over again, smirking at the woman's tears. When she pushed at his chest and tried to pull out of Neukirk's grip, Kyle punched Anna in the face several times. After climaxing he rolled off of her for Brandon who spit on her and raped her again.

## Chapter Thirteen

The ride to the Harold house was a welcome change for Bethel who had the two horses trotting merrily along the lane. The deep blue sky and billowy clouds could nearly convince her that the war was over and she was heading home. But a nice home cooked meal with Anna and her sister would be fine for now.

As she approached the house Billie Jean was in the side yard waving at her and smiling. Bethel brought the ambulance along the house and was confused at the change in Billie Jean's expression. She ran around to the rear of the wagon and nearly cried.

"I was hoping Anna had gone on to the camp and was with you. I thought she would be with you!"

Bethel hopped down from the driver's seat. "Why are you upset, Billie Jean? Anna has gone to town alone before."

"Something's wrong, I just know it. She walked to town over two hours ago and should have been back by now."

"Let me get the horses some water then I'll go look for her. Why didn't she take the buggy?" Bethel tried to sound reassuring.

"Oh, she likes to walk sometimes. I would feel much better if you'd find her, Tandy. We got alot of scum lurking around here since this goddamned war started! There's a bucket next to the barn if you wanna get water from the creek." She pointed to the red flecked barn behind them, its paint struggling to remain attached.

"Everything will be fine. You go sit in the porch swing and I'll fetch her." Bethel motioned with her hand toward the front porch as she hurried off to the creek bank.

The creek became ankle deep over a sand bar that Anna waded over. Her long hair fell loose around her shoulders and her dress hung open over one bare breast. A cut above her eyes bled profusely, bruises marked her cheekbones and around her eyes. She walked with her head down until she heard someone ahead. Anna had not realized she was that close to home. Tandy was filling a bucket full of water. She was suddenly ashamed of her appearance and tried to hide among the trees lining the stream.

"Anna?" Bethel slowly stood up, unsure of what she had just seen. Anna dropped to her knees in the water and covered her face. "Don't look at me!" She screamed.

Bethel ran along the bank until the brush became too thick then plunged into the knee deep water. The cold water churned with every step; the mud sucked at her boots. She approached Anna carefully and slowly.

"Oh God, don't look at me." Anna broke down completely, sobbing as if the world had ended.

Bethel knelt down beside her and gently fastened the buttons not torn off the dark blue dress with tiny white roses scattered like stars. She turned her head to the trees and away from the kind soldier.

"I don't want my sister and daughter to see me this way."

"Billie Jean sent me to look for you." She took a handful of cold water and washed the blood from Anna's face. "Let's get you out of this creek." Bethel's voice was soft, her grip gentle as she took Anna's hand.

Anna let out a deep sigh. She should have been terrified of a man, but there was something very different about Tandy Scott. Her heart told her that there was nothing to fear. "Well, I can't stay here all night can I?"

"Can I help you up?"

Bethel slipped an arm around Anna's waist and pulled her up then walked her to a portion of the bank where they could climb out. As they head toward the house Anna begins to cry again and runs behind a large oak tree near the barn.

"How will I ever live with this? I can't face anyone."

Walking slowly over to Anna, Bethel takes both of her hands. "You're not the one who should be ashamed. Will you tell me who should be?"

"Promise me that you and George will not kill them. Don't ruin your lives for the likes of that scum from hell." Anna's voice was firm.

"You are going to press charges. You can't let this lie."

"What good would it do? His daddy will just get him out of it and I don't know who the other son-of-a-bitch was, but Sims called him Brandon."

Bethel's jaw clenched tight. "It was Kyle Sims? What did this Brandon look like?"

Anna gazed up at the trees limbs as if the answers were written there. "He was tall, blue eyed, blonde and had the most condescending attitude of anyone I've ever met. And he wore an officer's uniform." She studied the soldier's face then slipped her arms around Bethel. "I see the fire in those pretty gray eyes. If you care for me, and I think you do, don't after them. Please."

Bethel swallowed hard, choking back tears. "They had no right. You're so kind, so gentle…."

"So are you, Tandy." Anna squeezed Bethel tight and sobbed on her shoulder for several minutes, then pulled back.

"I have to be strong for my little sister and daughter. I've had my cry and if you would fetch a bucket of water I'll wash up some more before we go into the house."

"I wish there was something I could do." A pained, helpless expression played on Bethel's features.

"You can help me look presentable so I do not scare the hell out of my three year old! Don't tell Billie Jean about the rape. Just let her think I was robbed. Please?"

"You don't think she is going to believe that, do you?"

That evening a small fire burned low in the fireplace as a cold front planted a chill in the air. Billie Jean rocked the toddler, Emma, near the fire with a displeased look on her face. She looked from Bethel smoking a pipe and leaning on the mantel to her sister, nursing a blackening right eye with a cold rag. "I can't believe that men would do that to you just for some cheese and jam."

Anna laid on the sofa trying to play down the pain she felt in every muscle of her body. "Some people know no bounds, Billie."

"We'll go into town and report those sons-of-bitches to the constable."

"Oh Billie, what would be the point? Horace Sims has everyone bought and paid for." Exhaustion weaved its way through Anna's tone.

"We could report Brandon to the Provost Guard; his money won't matter to them. At least you could have some justice." The gentle flickering of the flames softened the tones of the blue and white wall paper and the patterned furniture. It was an elegant room where one could nearly forget the war and the horrid rape of the mistress of the house. Bethel let a breath of smoke.

Billie Jean gave Bethel a doubtful look. "That won't work either."

Bethel bent over and knocked the burnt contents from her pipe into the fireplace then turned to the two sisters. "Why? It's their duty to act as military police. They don't look kindly on those that abuse their power on civilians."

Anna sat up. She studied the handsome soldier, touched by the naivety Tandy still maintained through all the terror of war. "Because Kyle Sims is a provost officer and. daddy's money goes a very long way around here. Maybe the provost guard is noble on the front, but in the rear they are despicable. Tandy, I think would like to sit on the porch a bit. Billie, could you put her to bed for me?"

Billie threw her sister a crooked grin. "I'm sure the night air will do you good. Why didn't you bring that nice cousin of yours with you?"

"George couldn't get a pass, but I will tell him that you asked after him." Bethel nodded and smiled.

As she stood up with the sleeping child Billie Jean looked back with mischief. "You be sure to do just that, Tandy Scott."

Anna draped a wrap around her narrow shoulders and went outside onto the porch with her guest not far behind. She sat in the far end of the porch swing and Bethel at the other end.

"The likes of Kyle Sims as a provost officer, I can hardly believe it."

Anna swung her legs slowly, making the swing sway gently. "They are a sorry lot; I can assure you of that much. What happened to me is not uncommon. If I didn't have little Ella to worry about I'd fill them both with lead." Anna reached out for Bethel's hand and held onto it.

"In some ways you remind me of my husband. Michael truly believed that most people were good and I used to see the same hurt in his eyes that I see in yours when people disappointed him. It was almost a surprised look.  What would he think now?"

Bethel squeezed Anna's hand. " I'm not surprised at anything a human being does anymore and Michael probably wouldn't be either. This war has changed everything and everybody. He wouldn't let them get away with it, I very much doubt that."

 "No, he wouldn't want to, but I would tell him what I told you. I believe that what comes around goes around."  Anna turned toward her friend with a stern expression. "You listen to me, Tandy! You have your whole life ahead of you. Don't throw it away on revenge." Anna rubbed a knot forming on her forehead. Her right eye was swelling shut and though she tries not to cry tears run down her cheeks.

The bruises on Anna's arms and face make Bethel want to hunt the son of a bitch down, but anger isn't making her heart pound and her hands sweat.  Even with the injuries Anna was beautiful. For the first time in her life Bethel wanted to kiss someone. As if she understood, Anna slid close and put her head on Bethel's shoulder. They held onto each other for some time before Bethel spoke. "You know what's funny? Me and George and our families back home don't have no use for the southern cause, whatever the hell it is. But it ain't healthy siding with the blue bellies either, so we joined the Confederate army to protect the folks back home. A bunch of those provost bastards killed my broth… cousin, Ed. They didn't mean to though; they was really there to hang my uncle for burning bridges that he didn't burn."

 Anna caught the slip of tongue and wondered silently what her companion had to hide. "Do you wish you had joined up for the Union?"

Bethel looked down at Anna. "Oh, that's dangerous talk. I think about it, probably too much. What happened today doesn't help my attitude."

"It's chilly out here tonight. "Anna snuggled into Bethel who pulled her closer.

Bethel was tense and scared of her feelings. She knew that this could not advance much further, that Anna would have to be told that Tandy Scott was really Bethel Erwin. But the sensation in her chest was so sweet and warm that she wanted to live in the moment.

"Let's pretend that today didn't happen and that you are not a soldier and neither one of us has to mend anymore wounds. Just for a few hours let's make believe that this war never started." Anna smiled up at Bethel.

Unable to help herself any longer, Bethel placed her lips on Anna's and they kissed slowly for several sweet moments until Billie Jean's giggling through the screen door made them stop.

"Oh, you wicked, wicked girl!" Anna said through a grin.

"I don't believe you have any room to talk, my dear." Billie winked then turned around and went into the kitchen.

## Chapter Fourteen

The next day Bethel, George and Tim sat around a small cooking fire at the camp outside Corinth. A chunk of desiccated vegetables lay at the bottom of a boiling pot of water.

Tim shook his head with a foul look. "I don't know what wise soul first called this mess desecrated vegetables, but I do salute him!"

"Hell, I rather have some damned salt horse. Shit, how much worse can it get?" George spit in the dirt.

Bethel reached into her pocket, brought out three potatoes and dropped them into the pot. "A little present from Anna."

Where is she today? I haven't seen her around anywhere." George asked as he monitored the boiling spuds.

Bethel chewed on a blade of grass and also studied the boiling water as if a great secret lie in its swirling pattern.

Tim smiled at Bethel. "She coming today? The boys around here miss her already."

She let out a breath then bit her lip. "I'm gonna tell ya something and you can't let Anna know that you know. I mean it, not a damned word!"

George gave her a funny look then busted up the dried ration in the pot. "So what happened?"

"It ain't just what happened, it's who did it. God, this is so hard to even say."

Tim reached out and squeezed her knee. "Come on, Tandy. It's just us."

"You know that piece of rabbit shit that teased her in town that one day?"

"Kyle Sims?" George let a belch to emphasize his opinion.

"You'll never guess you his buddy is-Brandon Neukirk."

"That pussy. What's he doing here, who's he with?" George stirred the pot.

Bethel took off her cap and ran a hand through her sweaty hair. The air felt good.

"He's an officer with the 29th Tennessee infantry."

Tim coughed loudly. His face gaunt and dark circles rode under his eyes. His uniform was dirty and his boots caked with mud. "They did something to Anna? " He asked softly.

It was necessary for Bethel to answer as both her brother and cousin understood her silence and pained expression. "You should see her poor face, the bastards."

George sighed deeply. "What about Billie Jean?"

"She's fine and thinks Anna was just beat up and robbed. She don't know about the rape and Anna don't want her too. She told me that she's going to send her daughter Ella out to her brother's place in San Francisco."

"Ever day since Ed was murdered I keep asking myself why I joined up, why I keep sleepin' in the mud, why I keep eating this crap!" He threw the spoon into the raging pot of water that had turned a soupy green. "I worry about ma and pa, wonder about who's in more danger, us or them and now this."

"I thought I was the only one having those feelings. What are gonna do about it?" Tim waited for an answer.

"Well, Anna don't want us doing anything. I can't let it go though." The anger in Bethel's eyes made them darker. George agreed that they could not stand by and let Sims and Neukirk treat women like dogs. The three soldiers discussed the purpose of war if the aftermath of battles never improved the quality of life or even made it worse.

"If Sims is provost, then he must hang around the train stations harassing people. Neukirk can't be allowed to see ya up close cause you know he'd give ya up. We gotta be careful, but accidents can happen around train stations." George flashes his two companions a knowing look.

Tim glanced around for anyone close enough to hear, but most of the other troops were concerned with cooking their own meals or were trying to wash down cornbread baked by the company cooks. "I'll help ya make things right for Anna, then I'm getting' the hell outta here. I'm sick. I won't live through winter this way."

"That's dangerous. Provost and conscription officers are everywhere looking for deserters to hang." Bethel replied in a harsh whisper.

Tim's expression was calm. "I don't have to go that far." George turned slowly to face Tim. "Are you saying what I think you are?" Tim smiled and looked down at his muddy boots.

Bethel put the kepi back on her head. "I've thought about it too. We only joined the Rebs to keep the folks back home safe and that didn't work. We wouldn't be the first to cross the lines."

"Oh shit, I don't know. If we get caught they'll shoot us." George had serious doubts about defecting, in spite of his previous bravado. "Then we'd best plan it good and quick before they ship us somewhere else!" Tim's stomach howled. "Are the damned taters done yet? I'm gonna starve to death before anybody can put a bullet in me."

"Who better to protect us than a whole army? At least the Yanks have tents and blankets and they're gonna win anyway." Pulling a hunting knife from her belt, Bethel stabbed one of the potatoes. It broke apart. Pieces of hydrated vegetables floated around on the surface. "I guess this shit is ready to eat." She broke up the rest of the potatoes.

Grabbing the ladle, Tim filled his tin cup with the soup and downed it like a hungry wolf. He slurped it with George watching in amazement.

"We'd better do it quick cause the talk is that we're going to evacuate Corinth real soon.  Everybody's got the runs and the generals don't want to face the Yank with sick soldiers. They got some troops sharpening stakes and digging ditches to slow Grant down. There's panic in the air." George commented as Bethel filled her cup.

"Where we gonna hide till we find some Blue Bellies?" Tim savored a chunk of potato.

"Anna has a cellar under the barn and I know she won't have an objection to us defecting."   She studied the reaction of her brother and cousin.

"We are talking about serious offenses. You don't have to go with us; they can't do anything to you for deserting."  George offered, knowing the response.

"I'll be changing uniforms with ya. You ain't getting rid of me now." Bethel quipped.

"Aren't we all noble? The two of you just don't want to run off and leave certain damsels in distress behind."  Tim smirked as he skipped the spoon and dipped his cup for a second helping.

*********************

Two nights later Kyle Sims was walking along a line of rail cars near the train station of the Memphis and Charleston line. He swung a baton while stopping nearly every soldier before boarding to check his furlough papers. It is raining and the men are irritated at being held up by a provost officer.

"I wanna see your papers!" Sims glared at a young man with tired eyes and sunken checks.

"I got a week leave. Got to heal myself up so I can be shot up and starved again." The private tried to keep his tone level.

A flash of anger tinted Kyle's eyes. "You sassing me? How would you like some time behind bars.

The private glared back at Sims. "It can't be any worse than I've already known. You should be glad that fellas like me just keep getting used up so that boys like you don't have to get their hands dirty!" The soldier came up close to Kyle and stuck a revolver in his crotch. "I don't fear dying for the cause, but I damned well won't die because I starved to death! Now, I'm getting' on that train and if you have any wish to sire offspring you will not interfere with that process."

Sims swallowed hard and stepped back slowly to let the private board the train. Humiliation and a foul mood painted his features. He quickly checked to see if anyone saw the incident, but in the chilly rain no one was paying any attention.

Another young soldier came out of the depot and Sims was on him like a barn owl on a baby rabbit. "What's your name?" Sims demanded.

The thin, blonde private was clearly underage, his fear apparent as he stood before Sims. "Miller, sir."

"Why aren't you with your unit, soldier?" The muscles in Kyle's jaw twitched rapidly.

"I have a pass, sir. My pa died and there's nobody to work the farm but my ma and sisters."

"Give it to me." Sims demanded and Miller reached into his pocket for the pass written on brown paper. The rain quickly darkened it and the ink ran. "I can't read this. Who are you with?"

"The 1st TN infantry, sir." He straightened just a bit.

"Get back to your unit. Your furlough is revoked." The Provost Guard had the power to revoke passes at will, something Sims truly relished. The younger man was surprised and a questioning expression lingered on his face. He wrote on the pass that it was revoked by the Provost Guard and shoved it back to Miller. "Now move out."

Miller's chin quivered as he thought of his family back home. He thought better of arguing with Sims as something about his demeanor made Miller believe he was capable of most anything. He turned and headed back down the road with thunder rolling in the dark clouds above.

\*\*\*\*\*\*\*\*\*\*\*\*\*\*\*\*\*\*\*\*

George Erwin walked a picket line outside of camp. The rain poured and the heavy clouds made the evening darker than usual. He ducked his head to keep the cold rain out of his face. At the sound of a wagon approaching Erwin jerked his head up. The wagon stopped and someone climbed down.

"Much obliged to ya." Miller shouted through the storm.

"No trouble at all. I don't know what's going on, but I seen more trains come through here lately than I've ever seen." The driver remarked.

"Can't say I know, sir. They tell us lowly privates anything." Miller waved as the driver began to turn the wagon around toward town. The driver looked to George who waved him on. Miller walked up to the line and stopped near George. "Identify yourself."

"Private Miller, 1st Tennessee."

"I need to see your pass!" The cold rain muffled Erwin's voice. Miller covered his pass with his hat. "Here's my furlough papers. Some asshole at the train station cancelled it for me. For no good reason."

George held the paper close to his face then smirked at the signature of Kyle Sims. "He shouldn't telling anybody what to do."

"You know that son of bitch?" Miller responded.

"I know all I need to know about that weasel. Come on through and try to find a way to get dry." George moved the barricade back enough to let him past.

"I was going to spend the night on a train, now it's back to a mud hole and that slimy damned oil skin." Miller patted Erwin's shoulder as he went by.

"There many people out tonight with the storm and all?"

Miller shook his head. "No, but it's got more to do with them provost mongrels than the weather. You try to stay awake now." The rumble of trains a short distance away mingled with the rolling thunder as George watched Miller walk toward the camp, the tent peaks appearing like waves in the flashes of lightening. Miller shouted and ran when the rain poured harder.

*****************

Three hours later at two in the morning Bethel, George and Tim crouched near some trees watching a long line of box cars pass as the train slowed down for the depot in Corinth. The heavy rain and lightening sent the guards inside the cars instead of manning the roof tops as usual. The three moved closer to the track as the old caboose came into sight. A dim lit flickered inside the car and smoke rolled from the stove pipe.

In a few quick strides George grabbed the hand rails on the caboose and pulled himself up. He immediately ducked down beneath the window and moved over to the far side of the platform to make room for his companions who swiftly followed. The interior of the car suddenly became brighter when one of the two soldiers inside stuck another log into the stove.

Bethel peered through the window to find one of the men sleeping and the other still bent over the open door on the stove. The wind changed direction and blew the cold rain horizontally from the east, nearly drowning them as dark shapes of buildings appeared through the mist. Stacks of barrels emerged outside a warehouse near the depot. She pointed toward them and George nodded his head.

In the depot office Kyle Sims sat close to a large potbellied stove with his feet up on some wooden crates. An officer named Dan Emert wandered in from another room.

"Go do another round." Emert stated bluntly, chewing on a stick. Kyle dropped his feet to the floor, frowning. "Sir, not even the stupidest Yank would be out tonight."

Captain Emert lit his pipe and took a few puffs; the yellowed tinted edges of his mustache bore testimony to a long time habit.

"It's not people getting' in that I'm worried about Sims. We got us a morale problem as you should know. Now, get on out there. The last train for the night just pulled in."

Sims pulled his hat on. "I hate cowards; they're a disgrace to the south!"

Emert took a few steps toward Sims and blew gray smoke in his direction. "Just what would you know about it? Your daddy bought you a ticket in the back of the theater."

Thinking better of mouthing off to this superior, Sims clamped his lips shut and charged out the door into the raging weather, blocking the rain from his face for hundred yards than dashed cursing into the warehouse. The interior was dark and he squinted around him as he removed his hat to shake the water off. Dim rows of shelves ran from floor to ceiling with many half empty from black market deals ran by Horace Sims. Kyle took off the damp coat and placed it on a nearby shipping desk. He searched the desk drawer and found a box of matches and lit the lantern hanging on the wall near the door. While taking it off the hook, Sims is immediately frightened by Bethel as she stepped in front of him. A hand clamped over his opened mouth and another stopped Kyle from drawing his side arm.

"One word and you die two minutes before we got planned." Bethel whispered with more venom than Sims had ever heard in his life. After fighting down the bile that crept up his throat, Sims mumbled through the fingers over his lips, "Take whatever ya want and get the hell outta here!"

George squeezed Kyle's face hard and twisted his arm behind up between his shoulder blades. Tim came up to tie a rag around his head and through his mouth, but Sims squinted hard at Bethel and spouted out, "I seen you before?"

"Well, I guess it's hard to recall things when you're so busy protecting innocent citizens." Bethel walked up close to him.

Sims suddenly smirked. "What? Oh, I see now. Your sweetheart told ya some sob story, but she begged for it fella. Widowed women have needs that boys can't fill, you know what I mean? No, you probably don't!" A hardy laugh prompted Bethel to kick him hard in the groin.

Tim slipped the rag through his mouth before Kyle could respond. His face was red and the veins in his neck pulled tight from pain. A gust of wind hit the door and Sims wet his pants. Bethel pulled a scalpel from her leather pouch. Its blade reflected the lantern light.

"You know what all us farm boys know how to do?" George grinned and looked to Tim. "Grab his legs."

Bethel cut the buttons from his fly then told them to flip him over. She grabbed his belt loops and yanked the trousers down to his knobby knees. Her two companions flipped Sims over as he struggled, tears running down his cheeks. "Settle down or I'll cut it all off, asshole."

She severed the scrotum neatly and quickly, the sharp blade cauterizing the wound. Only a few drops of blood hit the wooden planks of the floor. She motioned for them to lay him back down. With the skilled hands of a surgeon Bethel stitched up the incision. Sims went wide eyed then passed out.

"He dead?" Tim bent down over him.

"Hope not. I want him to live like that." Bethel wiped the blade off on Kyle's shirt.

"Just like de-nutting a pig." George remarked.

Bethel grunted. "Let's get outta here before somebody misses this shit."

## Chapter Fifteen

The next morning Lt. Zieman of the Provost Marshall's office strolled down the street with a newspaper under his arm still eating the cinnamon roll his wife made. He saw a package near the office door and increased his pace. There was a note on the small box wrapped in paper similar to butcher's wrap. Zieman unlocked the door then picked up the package. He dropped it on his desk. The first priority was to put coffee on for the day as nobody would work worth a damn without it. They were lucky to still have real coffee as the troops in the field were brewing chick peas and tree bark for their morning lift. After lighting the stove and putting the pot on a burner, Zieman finally sat down his desk and put the rest of the pastry in his mouth. He then read the note.

PROVOST PIGS RAPE OUR WOMEN, BUT NOT ANYMORE!

Zieman was confused as he opened the package, but suddenly understood as he unwrapped the rag in the box and saw two testicles. He spit the roll out all over the desk and cursed fiercely.

The night commander, Captain Emert, came through the door as Zieman filled the air with obscenities. He had a large envelope in his hand with his nightly report in it.

"Not a good sign when you're swearing like that at 7am." He tossed the report on the desk. "What the hell have you got there?"

"Christ!" Zieman jumped up. "Somebody's balls, that's what."

"Son of a bitch, I never thought we'd see them again." Emert pondered. Zieman gave him a strange look. "It's in my report. Kyle Sims went on his rounds last night and didn't come back. I sent some boys after him, figured he was sleeping or screwing some whore. They found him in the supply warehouse with those cut off."

"His father will have us all castrated for letting his baby boy be killed." Zieman paced the office.

Emert smiled. "Oh, he's not dead. Sims is in the hospital. Whoever removed his manhood damned well knew that he was doing." Emert lit his pipe. "Looks like the Sims name will die out. What a fucking shame."

"That isn't very funny, sir. He is one of our own."

"Please, even the surgeons said that with all the cracked heads he's sent their way they couldn't manage a tear. Sims gives us all a bad name." Emert took a few puffs then pointed at the box. "Feed those to the guard dogs. I'll go check in on our boy."

Sims was sweating profusely in a bed on the ward and fast asleep. A nurse wiped his face with a cool rag then excused herself as Emert and a tall, thin surgeon named Walters approached.

"He gonna make it?" Emert asked as Sims mumbled.

"More than likely. He has a slight infection from pissing himself and then crawling in the dirt. The sweating is from nightmares as the fever is low grade." The surgeon felt Kyle's pulse and nodded. "I think he'll be fine physically, but any other way who knows."

"Can't say as I've ever heard of this done to a man before." Emert studied Sims' face as it twisted in fear.

"Nor me, but I'm not surprised that somebody went after him. He ain't too popular around here." Walters turned toward another patient who moaned in pain. "I'd best get back to the wounded troops."

The slight against the provost guard wasn't lost on the captain. "In other words, you're saying there are many possible suspects in this matter." Emert looked up at the taller man.

"I got nothing against you, Captain, but you have some real scoundrels wearing that uniform and people fear them much as the Yanks." Walters gave instructions to a nurse then turned back to Emert. "Quite frankly, now my wife and daughters have one more reason to find the streets safer."

Emert smarted from the true, but stinging assessment of the guard. "I understand completely, doctor. I will do what I can to clean things up a bit."

Sims, who had been listening for the past few minutes, pulled himself up on his elbows. "You cock eyed son of a bitches. I'll get both of ya, you just wait." He winced and laid back down.

One of the patients near Sims laughed out loud and shouted. "Boy, you ain't got the balls!"

The ward erupted in jeers and clapping making Walters smile. It was the first time many of them had shown any sign of hope in weeks. "Well, I guess something positive can happen from everything." The surgeon looked around the ward and noticed even the sickest men were grinning.

"My father will……" Kyle tried to retort but passed out.

"Sure, whatever you were saying." Emert slapped the doctor on the arm.

"You know Horace Sims will hunt down whoever did this and it won't make any difference what side they are on. He was counting on grandchildren, a grandson I should say, to carry on the family name." Walters stated while looking over a patient chart. Emert grunted a reply. "Well, he's got one hell of a job then, and even if I knew who did it I wouldn't say a damned word. You know son, when you plant shit you reap turds." He winked at a young man with an amputated leg who smiled at Emert's words of wisdom.

\*\*\*\*\*\*\*\*\*\*\*\*\*\*\*\*\*\*\*\*\*\*

The white wicker chair that supported Horace's ample weight creaked as he tapped his foot. He sat at a small table on the porch of the Sims plantation house nursing a glass of peach brandy. Brandon Neukirk stood nearby with his new boot propped on another wicker chair, a shiny sword dangled at his side. Horace frowned deeply, his forehead a furrowed field of sweaty flesh.

"I feel your lose, sir. Kyle is a good friend and did not deserve the foulness inflicted upon him." Neukirk downed the last bit of his brandy.

"I want the sorry son of a bitch that castrated my boy then left him to die! What is this rapist shit all about?" Horace growled like a bulldog.

Brandon put his foot down and sat in the chair while Sims refilled his empty glass. "There was a woman in town that was very near throwing herself on Kyle. Not surprising considering what he stands to inherit."

"My boy does not have to rape anyone. Who the hell is she?" Small droplets of orange tinted alcohol clung to the edges of his mustache.

Neukirk took a mouthful of brandy trying to down play his alarm at Horace's question. It would not take long for him to learn the truth of what they had done to Anna Harold if he snooped around. "If you'll pardon me Mr. Sims, the less you know of this matter, the better. Let me handle the retribution aspect. A business man like you needs to be above reproach."

Sims studied his guest for a moment, analyzing the meaning then smiled. "I do appreciate the manners of a gentleman, Lt. Neukirk. Might I offer you a bit more before resuming your duties?" He placed a hand on the brandy bottle.

"Yes, sir I believe that I will.

# Chapter Sixteen

That next morning Anna Harold walked to her barn with a basket, watching all around her for anyone who might want to raid her house for what little she had left. There was panic in the air. She closed the barn door behind her and latched it, grabbed a lantern hanging near the door and lit it before lifting the trap door to the cellar.

The creaking of the door startled the three men below her huddles among the jars of fruits and vegetables. They squinted at the flame and jumped to their feet.

"It's just me. You can' come on out."

George, Bethel and Tim emerged slowly into the darkness of the barn.

"Something is happening in town today. It is utter chaos and the trains are running one after the other. They say the Yanks are coming." Anna told them, her voice stressed.

"We must be evacuating and retreating south." Bethel commented as she dusted off her pants.

Tim looked to his comrades. "That's good right? Good for us."

George had walked over to the barn door and was peering through the crack. "Maybe, but even the Yanks don't think much of traitors. We could be sent to prison."

Anna shook her head as she paced, her skirts swaying with her steps. "Then don't surrender to them."

"Listen, I think we can convince the blue bellies that we wanted to join them in the first place. We were afraid for our families and we had good reason to be." Bethel said calmly.

"One of us has to live long enough to go back home and you stand the best chance of that." George poked his sister with a stern look and she returned it. Anna looked to each of them with concern. "If you two join the Yanks then so will I! We can't go home; provost will be crawling the countryside looking for fresh troops and deserters." Bethel nearly shouted but Anna motioned her voice down with a flat hand.

"I'd rather take my chances with the Yanks. A prison shithole is better than rope around your neck." Tim's face was tinted yellow from the lantern flame. "God, why didn't you put windows in here?"

"We had livestock and as far as I know they do not need a view." Anna replied. "I have heard in town that the Union is signing up prisoners of war willing to take the oath and fight for them. They are short of troops as well."

George kept looking to his left as if he could see the house through the barn wall. "We heard the same thing, about Yanks taking on deserters. Joining up might be our only choice".

Anna smiled. "Go on, she's in the kitchen. Why don't we all go in the house? I think the army has its hands full in town. You can stay in the attic if you want for a few days, not in that dank hole. Tandy, would you help me for a minute?"

George grabbed Tim and opened the barn door. "Come meet Billie Jean." The men checked for spying eyes then darted for the house. Bethel watched her brother and cousin run for the back porch and Billie Jean opened the screen door for them. She avoided Anna's eyes until she took hold of Bethel's hands.

"I may never see you again and I wanted to tell you how much your friendship has meant to me." Anna's face was soft, her eyes full of sincerity.

"Me too. We're a long way from home and you've been very kind to us." Bethel felt a large lump in her throat and her heart pounded as she studied the dirt floor.

Anna placed a hand on Bethel's chin and pulled her face upward. "I have learned some hard lessons in this life. One is that there may not be a tomorrow and the other is that you must take joy where you find it. I love you; Tandy Scott and I'm terrified of never seeing you again."

"Oh Anna, you're so pretty, so sure of yourself. You deserve much better than me, I promise you. I am not who you think I am." Bethel felt a tear slide down her right cheek.

Anna reached up and caught it. "It has been a long time since I have been in love. And I don't even know your real name." Bethel was dumbstruck for a moment, and then realized that Anna had probably known her secret all along. Anna came close and kissed Bethel lightly near her mouth sending shivers down her spine. "Bethel, Bethel Erwin." She replied in a whispered tone.

Bethel returned the kiss slowly and softly until she felt like they were melting together, like there was no war going on and nothing mattered except the two of them clinging to each other. A wave of warmth came over her and Bethel hoped that no provost guard came through the door as she could not defend herself in this new, glowing state of euphoria. After years of wondering why so many songs had been written about love, the loss of it or unrequited love, Bethel now fully understood the obsession.

"I love you, Anna. I won't ever let anybody hurt you again. I wish I could stay with you, God what I would do to have life be normal again."

"It's going to tear my heart out to see you leave here, but I know you have to go. Let me pack you all something to eat before you set out. If might be awhile before you find the right people to surrender to, some let's go to the house."

Bethel followed Anna to the house with a strange stirring in her loins and a deep longing she didn't comprehend. Why had she never felt anything like this before? Fate picked one hell of a time for emotional upheaval.

That night in the attic George and Bethel lay near the small open window talking in whispers. Tim was curled up under the eave with his head on a piece of old blanket. Bethel told George about what happened in the hopes that he might have some wisdom to offer since he had dated in the past.

"Are you mad?" He hissed. "You can't encourage her like that. I know you're not like other girls, but you can't do that either!"

"I've never felt anything like it. Now I know why you always acted so stupid around Pam Neukirk." Bethel grinned.

George flicked her on the ear. "I guess you can hope you don't see her again, but if we hitch up with a Yank unit near here we could be in Corinth a lot longer. Wonder if I get serious about Billie Jean? Wonder if I even marry her? The truth will have to come out."

"My you're putting the cart before the horse, but I know, I know. I just never considered that love would be a part of my life." She smiled as a cool, sweet breeze caressed her face, reminding her of Anna.

"Well, you have to honest about the whole thing. You know how people are, Bethel". George's tone softened.

Tim rolled over and grumbled. "Will you two shut the hell up? Oh, and ask them if they have another sister for me. I always knew you was a three legged dog, Bethel." He chuckled.

"Asshole." She whispered with a grin.

"Let's try to get some sleep. We got some uncertain times ahead of us." George stated looking somber, and then farted to ease the tension. They all laughed, but they all were also scared about venturing out away from the sanctuary of the Harold household. Until they actually signed on the dotted line for the Union, they had no friends.

## Chapter Seventeen

The night of May 30, 1862 the city of Corinth lit up the sky as bonfires burnt homemade knives and supplies were torched to keep the Union from confiscating them. The horizon was painted an orangey glow behind silhouetted trees tops. Confederate troops rushed to board retreating trains that would take them deeper south, further way from the advancing enemy. From several miles away the sound of trains rumbling on rails and whistles blowing as engines departed could be heard, but the confusion, shouting, screaming and stark fear of a deserting army were muffled in a sleepless night. Anna Harold lay in her poster bed listening for sounds of an intruder. The stillness was heavy like black ink; the air was too warm for comfort. She startled when Billie Jean announced that she was going to the outhouse and then refill the water bucket. Anna told her to be careful and hurry, and then went to her bedroom window to watch her for sister.

Billie Jean soon emerged from the back porch with a lantern in one hand and a shotgun in the other as she darted to the rear of the house toward the creek to the outhouse. It was then that Anna smelled burning wood and heard the crackling of fire. She ran to the window on the south side and saw the flames licking the air as it fed on her house. Acrid smoke floated through the window like a dense fog. Screaming her sister's name, Anna ran down the stairs out the front door.

The sound of a shotgun blast and Billie Jean calling out an insult preceded her running to the pump and grabbing one of the spare buckets that hung on a pole.

"Come on! Help me get that fire out. I think we still can." Billie Jean shouted as she filled the bucket with water while furiously working the handle. She took off before her sister could answer.

Anna also filled a bucket, but the fire was on the far side of the house and she felt heartsick. There was no way they could save the house, yet doing nothing seemed like a sin. When she joined Billie Jean the entire south side was covered in raging flames that seemed angry as they devoured the Harold house.

"The son of a bitch! He threw something on it, oh God. We'll lose everything" Billie Jean started to cry. "Let's try to save some of it."

"No, we'll both be killed. It's burning too hot. You saw somebody?" Anna grabbed Billie Jean's hand and pulled her far from the house.

"Some horse's ass wearing a uniform. I scared the hell out of him though and he took off through the woods." She pointed to the dense trees a short distance from the house.

Anna knew it had to be one her rapists hoping to silence her forever in case the Union won the war. Survivors had long memories.

*********************

Major Merriweather of the 58th Illinois Infantry sat in his tent at a folding table going over maps and recent scouting reports. It was late evening and his eyes were tired from reading by lantern light. He was interrupted by a corporal who approached with a group of prisoners.

"Sir, we found these rascals crossing the river. Claim they seen the light and want to join up with us." The corporal's uniform was soaked from the excursion and his wet hair was pasted to his skull.

Putting down the pen, Merriweather ducked under the tent top to inspect the latest bunch of deserters. The northern army also had its share of deserters, but Lincoln had the idea that the army could be strengthened if prisoners would agree to fight for the Union.

The major cleared his throat. "My corporal, the south must be in dire straits." He clasped his hands in the center of his back and walked slowly around the captured group. One man looked him in the eye. "Son, do we know each other?" Merriweather asked.

"Not exactly sir, but we did hear you speak at our church back home near Longmire, Tennessee. You were a captain then." George was terrified and struggled to keep his voice from shaking.

"Oh, yes. I found myself alone at that train station as I recall. I could have used your company then." The major spoke slowly, peering down at the shorter man.

"We would much rather have joined up with you, but we were afraid of what might happen to our families. Rebs killed my little brother, Major. This here is my cousin, Tandy and my cousin Tim. The Rebs also raped Tandy's fiancée, so you see we don't owe nothin' to the South. We're all ready to swear allegiance to the Union." George Erwin faced the officer bravely, his bouncing Adam's apple the only obvious sign of fear.

Bethel and Tim voiced their agreement and Bethel grinned slightly at the word "fiancée".

The major studied the pathetic looking men. "You know that most prisoners of war are either sent to prison camps or paroled back to their regiments…" He let the words sink in and saw their sick expressions. "But, I believe you. I was there and know that you didn't have much choice. I understand the plight of those from eastern Tennessee. The fact that you did not desert and head for home is in your favor, boys You realize that you might be shooting at people you know?"

Bethel pushed her hair back under the dirty cap. "Our families are living under martial law and the south is going to lose the war. That is our reality, sir."

"We'll be the best soldiers you've got cause we got something to prove." George stated with true valor.

"You're damned right! While I was out here crapping my guts out, some asshole stole my families pigs and chickens and anything else they wanted." Tim piped up.

Merriweather studied his pale, clammy skin. "You can go to sick call in morning. Any of you have any special skills?"

George placed a hand on his sister's shoulder. "Tandy worked with the surgeon and is damned good."

"That right?" The major appeared interested.

"Yes, sir. I've done about everything there is to be done to a wounded man." Bethel shook off the exhaustion and pulled herself up straight.

"We're both good shots and know how to handle a sticker." George pointed to himself and Tim.

Pacing back and forth Merriweather nods to a sergeant that joined them. "They need to take the oath and then get them uniforms and shoes; the ones they've got are pathetic. You'll all need to speak with the intelligence officer. He'll be very interested in what you have to say. If he thinks you're spies you'll be strung up from the nearest tree. I'll take care of the paperwork. That will be all. You are dismissed."

Sgt. Jack Williams threw the group a disgusted glare. "Jesus, isn't it bad enough that I got to deal with Yanks, but now I got a bunch of Johnnies that look like they crawled out from under a rock! Get moving before I throw ya back like runty perches."

The march through camp brought whistles and name calling from the Union troops cooking, cleaning weapons or playing instruments. Bethel felt her face grow hot at the insults as some spit at them or tossed rocks.

"I sure feel like we done the right thing." George whispered to Bethel.

"Least we're still breathin'." She retorted.

It was a long evening with each of them having to be interrogated by Captain Mark Henson alone. After he was convinced the three were not spies, Henson sent them to the mess tent for chow, which was somewhat better than what the Rebs served but not by far. They wolfed down supper then were taken to a tent with uniforms and shoes piled on the ground.

It took half an hour to find shirts, caps and shoes that fit acceptably, but Bethel's shoes were too big. She couldn't find any paper to stuff in them as paper was a commodity with every scrap used to write home on. George found some rags near the mess tent that were dirty but filled the gap between her toes and the shoe tips.

At eight o'clock the three were joined by six other former Confederates to take the oath and swear allegiance to the Union. Sgt. Williams stood before the troops with his right hand held up and told them to do the same. He would make a statement and the men were to repeat it. Bethel did not recognize any of the other Rebels. One was very tall with large feet and he still wore his old tattered shoes. At least she could make hers fit.

That night the nine new Union soldiers slept near each other as it would take some time to be completely trusted and welcomed, if that were to ever occur at all. They lay on the ground under a starry sky wondering what the future had to offer. Exhaustion soon over took Bethel and she slipped off to a dreamless sleep.

# Chapter Eighteen

The next morning Union troops approached the outskirts of Corinth to find ditches dug along the northern edge with sharpened poles protruding from the trenches. It was an attempt to slow down the advance as the southern army retreated. There were no signs of healthy white men in the streets. The only males visible were young boys, old men and Negroes. Any men capable or willing to fight them had fled.

Piles of burnt debris were everywhere with smoke still swirling from structures torched to prevent the Yanks from possessing them. Major Merriweather rode up along side Bethel and George on a white mare. Tim had been held back at sick call. "Lieutenant, take this squad and let them show you where the enemy storied their supplies. I doubt that anything will be left, but search for stragglers too. These two men can help you with that." The major spoke to an officer riding ahead of the troops.

"Yes, sir." Lt. Harding turned and gave Bethel and George a scornful expression. He had no use for traitors one way or the other. "You men follow me."

Riding at a fast trot Harding forced the squad to double quick time after him. A few minutes later the depot and burnt warehouse came into view. Negro men emerged from the ruins with arms full of supplies they could salvage.

"Put that merchandise down! That is property of the United States Army." Harding shouted harshly and placed his hand on his sidearm when the men hesitated. They dropped the goods and ran.

"Don't hardly seem worth it." Bethel commented upon seeing that the goods were damaged and smelled heavily of smoke.

Harding turned his horse around. "You're lucky it was Merriweather they brought you to as to me you are just plain old traitors. Your people let the city go to women, children and niggers that ran off like whimpering dogs. Get your asses in there and secure that building!"

George thought of making some remark then reconsidered. He followed Bethel into the blackened skeleton that seemed like a gateway to hell with the heat and smoldering wood. The acrid smoke makes the soldiers cough.

A young Negro boy startled Bethel when he sprinted from behind a pile of rubble and bumped into her. He then darted out the back door toward the tracks. "Son of a bitch." Bethel grabbed her chest."He scared the shit outta me."

The lieutenant rode around the building and snatched the boy up by his suspenders. "What's your name, boy?"

The child hung in the air like a sack of flour with his toes barely touching the ground. "Josiah."

"Well, Josiah, if you wanted to rob the richest house in town where would you go?" Harding watched the boy swing back and forth in this grip as he tried to keep his balance.

"That be easy, sir. Colonel Sims is the richest man round here. He has a cellar under his big ole house and it stuffed full of all kinda things." The child winced as his pants pulled up tight.

"And just how would you know that?"

Josiah perked up. "Cause my mamma's sister is a cook for Massa Sims and he sold my cousins off just cause he didn't want 'em no more. She tell her whole family about that secret room."

George and Bethel listened at the door when they heard the name Sims.

"Well then it can't be much of a secret any more can it?" Harding remarked snidely.

"Oh yes sir it is! We don't tell nobody." The boy answered as Harding pulled him up on the saddle.

"You're gonna show us where it is. Scott, Erwin, go back around and fetch the wagon. We're going on a trip. The rest of ya follow me."

\*\*\*\*\*\*\*\*\*\*\*\*\*\*\*\*\*\*\*\*

The chard blackened timbers of Anna's house smoldered in the morning breeze. She wandered among the burnt boards that were once living room walls. One half of the second floor still stood with her bedroom opened up to the world, the pink and white of her bed quilt was dirty but the pattern was visible. The furniture and most everything else in the living room was useless. The sound of pots and pans banging preceded Billie Jean stepping over fallen timbers from the kitchen. She tossed the cooking utensils out onto the grass. "You know who did this?" She asked Anna who removed a framed photograph of her late husband from the fireplace mantel.

"Knowing doesn't make it any better, besides now Horace Sims has to deal with the Yanks." Using the corner of her sleeve Anna wiped the soot from Michael's image.

Surveying the smoldering inferno Billie Jean let out a deep breath. "What are we gonna do now?"

Anna pulled up a blackened, but fairly sturdy chair and perched on the edge of it. "I have no idea, Billie. We can stay with the Cohen's for a while to decide what to do next. I wonder where God goes when He's really needed?"

"Anna!" Billie Jean retorted having never heard her sister speak like that in the past.

Standing up slowly, Anna peered up through the skeletal roof with tears in her eyes. "Well, have you seen Him lately?"

The Sims Plantation bore the title, Sweetbriar. The long road up to the three story white house was lined with Weeping Willow and Magnolia trees. Before reaching the main house one saw slave quarters, a smoke house, a laundry shed and the foreman's residence.

Inside the main house the servants were hustling to and fro to the orders of Horace and his wife, Pamela who was forty-five and somewhat plump. Her tone was sharp with the slaves as they packed their valuables into boxes. The butler, Hansen, gathered up the silver candle sticks. A white beard gave him a dignified appearance. His manners were genteel like his father and grandfather who had grown up at Sweetbriar and were also butlers there.

      The Sims family had sectioned off a portion of the cellar and filled it with bedding, dry goods, candles, weapons and ammunition in case the South should fall. The door to the cellar from the house was disguised as a bookshelf. A young slave named Nathan was fixing the pump that was supplied through pipes from the spring house. He grinned when water came gushing out into the large sink. Abby had been bringing necessities down the narrow stairs since before dawn. "Ole Horace really think theys gonna hide down here forever? If he's that scared of them Yankees why don't he just pack up his kin and move?" She said in a low voice.

Nathan chuckled. "And leave all this behind?"

"And put that box in the secret room too. Hurry, those barbarians from the north will be here soon enough!" Pamela Sims shouted to Abby as she went back up the stairs.

"Don't seem right that poor folks got to face the Yanks along." Abby replied, pushing the red and white checked scarf far up her forehead. "Whenever trouble knocks it's always the poor that got to answer the door." Nathan took a handful of water and saw that it was muddy, so he kept pumping until the water cleared up.

Pamela Sims shouted down the stairs. "That's the last of it. Come up here now, all of you."

Hanson looked down at Abby and Nathan and motioned for them to make haste. "We're all here, Mrs. Sims."

Pamela is sweating and nervous. "I want the three of you to wait in Hansen's cabin until I give you further orders. Go on now."

Horace Sims came down the large, curving staircase made of maple. "You heard the Lady of the house!" He barked loudly.

Hansen takes his two companions by the arm and pulls them through the pantry out a side door. The situation was bad and nothing like he had ever experienced before. His cabin was the closest to the main house and they were inside in a few minutes. Two years earlier his wife had died and their one son had been auctioned off twenty years ago, so Hansen had the place to himself.

"I don't be liken this. Something ain't right!" Abby's eyes were wide.

"Lord girl, you always be distrustin' somebody." Nathan replied, though he was just as scared. He went to the window and watched from the side as a tall young white man approached with Horace Sims.

Abby whispered. "Who is it?"

"It be the Night Witch herself and her dark companion." Hansen answered her as he parted the curtains. The man with Sims was Brandon Neukirk without his uniform. "Get back." The older man waved for the two people to get away from the windows.

Nathan and Abby stood by the small table and chairs as the door burst open. Neukirk and Sims drew military issue pistols, making Abby gasp and move toward the back wall.

Hansen stepped up to them. "Master Sims, how can I help you sir?" Neukirk answered by pointing his revolver at Nathan and pulling the trigger. The bullet sank into the middle of his chest. With a surprised expression on his face he dropped to his knees.

Abby ran screaming to him. "Why? Why? We have always done whatever you asked us to do!"

"Masta Sims, what did we do wrong?" Hansen inquired only trying to buy time. They knew about the secret room and would not be allowed to live.

"Don't sass me! I got no choice. You three know too damned much." Sims growled at him.

Sims shot Hansen as he was backing away and Abby picked up a chair and threw it through a window. She plunged out the broken window and rolled in the dirt. Neukirk ran out of the shack after her and fired at Abby several times as the disappeared into a corn field. He followed her until reaching the far edge of the field where the crops ended and the land overlooked Corinth. Abby collapsed a few yards ahead of him and rolled limply down the hill. Brandon began to plunge down the grade after her but stopped as Union soldiers approached with a wagon.

\*\*\*\*\*\*\*\*\*\*\*\*\*\*\*\*\*\*\*\*\*\*\*\*\*\*

Harding approached the Sims house with the child talking nonstop, much to the amusement of the troops following them who feel rejuvenated in their new uniforms and shoes. Bethel's old uniform had become more dust than cloth.
"My feet hardly know what to do without holes in my shoes!" George strutted along near Hardings' white horse.
Another prisoner of war, Jim Esther, marched with Bethel. Esther was from an Alabama peach growing family with tousled brown hair that never seemed to lie down. "Think yer feet got a surprise, my gut almost up and quit workin' when real food down there!"
"We did the right thing......" Bethel started.
"Will you men shut the hell up? I don't what who is worse, the boy or you scum suckers." Harding turned in the saddle and threw them a menacing glare.
"It must take somethin' special to become an officer." George mumbled.
"You just became my official latrine digger, Erwin." Harding responded right before Josiah shouted and pointed to a splash of color on a distant hillside.
"There she is, Aunt Abby!" The boy tried to squirm off the horse, but Harding told him to stop.
"That's enough! Settle down and we'll ride on over." Harding looked back on his men. "All of you get in the wagon and quick time that damned horse."

**Chapter Nineteen**

In the hidden portion of the cellar the Sims couple crowded together on one of two beds in the small room. Their most valuable possessions were crammed into the room with them and Neukirk sat on the floor facing the door holding a Remington Army revolver given to him by Horace Sims.

Pamela Sims' eyes were red rimmed from crying. "I never dreamed that you would kill them. What kind of savages have we become?"

Her husband cleared his throat, the pressure of his wife's disapproval made him sweat. "Our preservation for the future was my first priority! You truly believe that those nigras would exhibit loyalty when those Union troops stomp their way across the front lawn?"

Brandon Neukirk turned toward Pamela. "Your husband is right, Mrs. Sims. We had no choice….but it is a thing I will find hard to live with."

Horace put an arm around his grieving wife. "I am not without feeling my dear, but times are strained. Brandon and I will go back up stairs and give you a chance to rest."

Getting to his feet Brandon extended his hand to Horace. "I cannot thank you enough for your help."

Pamela dabbed away her tears with an embroidered handkerchief. "You are a good friend to my son and we do remember our friends."

*********************

George carried the wounded slave, Abby up to the front porch of the Sims plantation house. He held her as Harding pounded on the ornate door.

"Open this door now! This is the United States Army and we are confiscating this property."

Bethel peered through the large window near a wicker chair and table. "I don't see in there, Lt. It looks like they've moved out."

"More like run off. You and Esther go around back and bust the damned door down. I don't think that I can get through these heavy doors."

The two soldiers ran to the backyard where they discovered a rear door somewhat less decorative than the front, but every bit as well made. Bethel kicked the door hard and it barely budged, which made her mad, so she then bashed the door lock with the butt of her rifle until it gave and the knob fell off. It rolled around in a little circle, the bright sun light making it sparkle like a child's toy.

"Here, let me throw my weight against it. I worked at Andersonville for six months, so I think I've been eatin' better than you." Esther was several inches taller and weighed some fifty pounds more than Bethel.

As she stepped aside, Jim plunged through the door sending it smacking the wall behind it. He fell into the closet door that concealed the secret entrance to the cellar's hidden room. Horace and Pamela Sims were halfway up the stairs listening to the ruckus when the man falling against the door scared them and they turned to go back down.

"Jesus, Esther, tear the whole damned house down!" Bethel grinned, but clearly impressed with his strength.

He chuckled while rubbing his shoulder. "I'll check this side of the place and you go that way, then we'll open the front for ole hard ass."

Bethel nodded and turned right down a hallway while Jim headed for the kitchen. Harding again pounded hard on the front door. She called him a name under her breath as she tried to concentrate on searching the rooms in the corridor. There was a sewing room, a sitting room and an office with fine wood furniture. It did not appear that the house had been abandoned very long. "Hey, somebody open the damned door!" The lieutenant screamed. "Private Scott my arms are not made of iron!" George hollered to his sister.

Bethel went through the parlor into the foyer and opened the double doors for her brother and Harding. The other five troops with them had spread out and were guarding the access road. George rushed past her and placed Abby on a sofa in the parlor. Josiah, who had not been in the main house before, looked around in awe. "Tandy! She's been shot in the chest, there's pink bubbles coming out." George shouted.

After leaning her weapon against a table Bethel dropped down to one knee near Abby. Her cotton dresses sported a widening red circle of blood on the left side and pink foam oozed from the wound.

"She caught a bullet in the left lung." Bethel ripped the hole in the dress wider and felt a sucking chest wound. "I've seen something tried in the field…I need cloth for a bandage, a candle and matches." George and Jim scattered then returned with the requested items. Bethel took a dish towel from Esther and cut a piece from it, then took the matches and candle from her brother. She laid the section of cloth over the wound and stretched it tight. After lighting the candle Bethel dripped wax all around the cloth border which pulled the injured ribs upward. The bubbled ceased and Abby's breathing became stable.

"I'll be damned." Harding leaned over Bethel. "I never seen anything like that before."

"Tandy's a natural born healer and a real quick learner, Sir." George beamed at such a prime example of family intelligence.

"That so Scott?" Harding asked her as he straighten. The soldier shrugged in response. "Well, I don't believe in wasting talent and neither does Captain Merriweather, expect a reassignment. What else to we need to do for this woman?"

Abby opened her eyes and squinted at the handsome man looking down on her. "Who are you?"

Josiah beamed at her voice and ran over to his aunt's side. "Aunt Abby."

"Child what is all this?" Abby winced as she tried to move her left arm to take her nephew's hand.

"We're from the U.S. Army. If it hadn't been for you nephew we wouldn't have found you when we did." Bethel explained while putting a hand on her right shoulder to keep her from getting up.

The lieutenant walked around to where Abby could see him. "Where are the people that own this house?"

The former slave appeared confused and rubbed her head as she thought. "They shot us…all of us who knew."

"About the room behind the cellar, the boy told us." George smiled at Josiah.

"Horace Sims and that no good friend of his son's shot me, Nathan and Hansen because we built that damned place so they could put all the goodies in the house down there. I never did dream they would kill us for it."

"Anyone care to guess where are missing hosts are?" Esther looked down at the floor.

"Then they've probably heard every word we have said here." Harding frowned.

"No, no. The secret room is behind the stairway on the other side of the house. There's a hidden door to it in the closet." Abby spoke slow and quiet.

"Any other way down to it?" The officer asked.

"Through the cellar entrance outside, there's a door behind some shelves." Abby winced in pain and appeared exhausted.

"All right now, that's enough talking. Sir, she needs some water." Bethel stood up prepared to go fetch some for her patient.

Harding held up a gloved hand. "Before any of us goes for water we need to take care of the problem. Erwin and Esther, you two wait by the closet door. We'll make a great deal of noise pulling off the shelves so that the occupants will run out the closet exit into your arms and we'll bring up the rear."

"You stay here with your aunt and don't move from this room." Bethel instructed Josiah with a firm tone. The boy stood next to the sofa and nodded his head.

George watched from the back door near the closet as Bethel and Harding each yanked opened the cellar doors. Drawing his pistol Harding peered down into the stairwell. He waved it at Bethel for her to go first and she did not hesitate, bringing a frown to her brother's face. Officers were chickenshits. When Bethel vanished into the ground George quietly opened the closet door.

The cellar, which was longer than Bethel expected, was bathed in shadow. There were shelves of canned vegetables and fruit on both sides and at the end where Abby said there was a hidden door. She stood to one side and waited for Harding who suddenly seemed in no hurry for confrontation.

On the other of the shelves Brandon Neukirk listened intently to sounds coming from the cellar.

Pamela Sims whispered. "Are you sure you killed them all? No one else should know about this room?"

Horace appeared irritated, nodded his head and put a finger to his lips to keep his wife quiet. The sound of creaking wood pulled Horace's eyes to the door to the cellar. Neukirk motioned the Sims couple up the other stairway into the house. They began a cautious assent up the stairs to the kitchen pantry door.

To surprise the intruders, Neukirk carefully undid the latch and kicked the door open to stare into the bearded face of a young Union soldier. He squinted at the familiar features. "Erwin? Be…"

She shot him in the heart. Neukirk dropped to his knees and fell backwards hitting his head on the floor. His pistol went off sending a Minnie bullet into Bethel's calf.

Bethel bent in half with the pain. "Damn it to hell!"

Soon another shot rang out and Horace Sims tumbled down the stairs, dragging his screaming wife with him. George kicked his way past Sims' body as he grabbed Pamela's arm and pulled her over to the bed in the corner. Esther came down after them taking the steps two at a time.

Harding helped Bethel limp over to a chair. "What did he call you? Did you know him?"

"Name is Neukirk; he was just some asshole from back home. He must have took me for George."

George threw his captive onto the bed where she bounded off and hit the brick floor. Pamela sobbed and kept looking at her dead husband.

"Is there anybody else in here?" George growled, hoping to scare any lies out of her.

"No! He was a good man....He was just looking after his family." Pamela gestured at the lifeless from of Horace Sims

Esther snickered. "We've seen your old man's handiwork lady, so spare us." Jim glanced around the small room filled with gold candle sticks, silver and crystal ware. "So this is what you killed those people over? Guess what, you rich bitch, one of them lived!"

The sound of Bethel groaning sent George over to his sister. "Are you hurt badly?"

She clenched her teeth. "No, hurts like hell though."

"You're bleeding too much to wait for treatment. Erwin, take Scott and the colored woman up stairs to the hospital in town and then return to camp. Bring back another wagon and two more men. Have Esther help get you get the two of them in the wagon." Harding ordered.

Deciding it was easier to take Bethel out the cellar door; George helped her up and pulled her arm around his shoulder as she hopped through the narrow threshold.

# Chapter Twenty

The jostling of the wagon made Abby grimace in pain as Bethel sat next to her in the wagon bed holding a bandage tightly on the wound.

"Just a little while longer, I know it hurts." Bethel comforted her though the searing pain in her right leg made her eyes water with every bump.

Abby smiled kindly. "You're such a nice boy, all concerned over me when you got a bullet of your own tormenting you."

"It doesn't hurt so bad now." Bethel gave the woman a reassuring grin than shouted to George driving the wagon. "George, when we get to the hospital I'm not getting out. We'll leave Abby and you take to Anna's place. I don't want anyone else tending to me."

Abby began to hum as George peered backward at his passengers. "That Tandy is a ladies' man. A real heartbreaker! Anna is one fine looking woman."

Abby smiles broadly and winked at Bethel, her voice growing hoarse. "She sure is."

A flash of fear colored Bethel's face. How did she know?

A few minutes later the wagon pulled up to the hospital entrance. George ran in and returned with a steward to help carry Abby to the rear section for colored patients.

"What about that soldier with ya?" The steward asked.

"Not serious. He's got orders to report back to camp." George replied as a doctor pointed out a vacant bed for Abby.

"Too bad for him, could have had a few days laying on his ass." The steward chuckled.

George signed some papers the ward steward gave him. "Oh, he'll be sitting on his ass working for the cook. Don't feel sorry for Tandy. "

The ride outside of town was just as unpleasant as the trip through Corinth, even with George trying to be gentle. Bethel sat with her back against the wagon front and held her leg stable. George started to sneeze as the smell of burnt wood filled the air near the Harold farm. "Jesus, they burned clear out here."

Bethel struggled to view the house through the trees, hoping that what she could see was not true. As the charred remains came into view Bethel's mood darkened. "Oh God, they burned the house down! Hurry!"

In the bright sunlight the blackened ruins seemed out of place and unreal among the green grass and trees. He pulled the wagon close to the destroyed living room as the front porch had collapsed. Bethel scooted to the edge of the wagon, cussing with each movement.

"What are you doing?" George asked.

"I gotta know if they're in there!" Bethel's voice was filled with dread.

"So do I, but you can't walk. I'll go look. Will you let me do that?" He sometimes wanted to smack her for being so independent and stubborn.

He grabbed onto a framing timber and pulled himself up into what was left of the living room. Wandering slowly through the rubble George was afraid of what he might find then noticed a chair in which the soot on it was smeared.

"They're not in here. I can't be sure, but it looks like someone sat in this chair after the fire." George jumped onto the grass and went over to where Bethel sat on the wagon with her good leg hanging off of it. He gently pulled her pant leg up past her wounded calf.

"Whoa, there's a lot of bruising."

"I can see that much! Go get me some water so I can rinse this blood off. I can't see a damned thing." She did not have much experience being a patient and it irritated Bethel to be dependent on anyone.

George ran to the pump and stuck a bucket under it, working the handle until water gushed out and overflowed the bucket. The barn door being ajar caught his attention. Feeling hopeful that the two sisters might be in the cellar he dashed back to the wagon and poured the water over Bethel's lower leg.

"I'm gonna check the barn, the doors are open!"

"Go, go, I'll tend to this." She told him while rubbing the dirt and blood from the wound.

As she cleaned the area Bethel watched her brother run to the barn and disappear inside. Her heart pounded as she studied her leg for an exit wound. What would George find inside? Visions of two terribly burnt women lying on the straw covered floor haunted Bethel as the next few minutes seemed to drone on for an eternity. Suddenly George appeared, excited and waving a piece of paper in his hand as he sprinted across the grass toward his sister. When he made it to the wagon his face looked like a child's on Christmas morning. Bethel read it out loud.

"Tandy, if you get back this way we are all staying with the Cohen's in town. We are fine, very angry and tired but in good health. Tell George that Billie Jean sends kind thoughts his way. Love, Anna"

One side of Bethel's mouth crept into a grin as she gave the note back to George. He read it again and let out a yell of joy, then remembered that Bethel still had a wound to treat and looked down at it.

"The bullet is still in there. I can't let a surgeon get that close to me. What the hell am I gonna do now? You have to get back to camp."

"I could just take you to back to town then go onto camp to fetch the other wagon and men. I'll just tell Harding you wanted your honey to tend to it." George batted his eyes like a woman.

"Wise ass. Want me to give Billie a message for you?" Bethel stated as she swatted flies from the still bleeding wound. She didn't much care for being on the patient side of the question.

"You just tell her that I am very happy that she is alive and well and that I will see her soon!" He beamed like any nineteen year old should when meeting a new love.

\*\*\*\*\*\*\*\*\*\*\*\*\*\*\*\*\*\*\*\*\*\*\*\*

At the Cohen house Bethel stood on one leg holding onto a bookshelf. Blood dripped onto the floor boards from the leg wound. She watched as Anna and Mr. Cohen hurriedly cleared a table for her to lie down on.

"When you are through I will carry him up the stairs to the guest room." Cohen peered at Anna over his narrow glasses.

Bethel heard that and shook her head. "No, you don't have to do that, I can…"

"Nonsense! You're nothing but skin and bones; it will be no trouble at all." The old man's tone indicated that it was the end of the argument, and Bethel was becoming too drained to bother trying to win it.

"Don't argue, Tandy. Carl, I need some of that lint we had left over and a bandage. A bowl of water and the sharpest knife you have." Anna wrapped a full apron around her dress.

Carl nodded and disappeared through the kitchen door. Anna leaned down close to Bethel's strained face and whispered. "Why on Earth did you not let George take you to the hospital? This is going to really hurt Tandy, this isn't necessary."

The compassionate expression on Anna's face brought tears to Bethel's eyes. "We can talk about this after you get this bullet out of me." She suddenly felt calm after Anna kissed her on the cheek. "Just relax and let us help you. Not after everything you have been through let someone else led the way."

"I've done things you cannot possibly imagine, Anna. Believe me." Mr. and Mrs. Cohen rush around closing up the store and retrieving rags and lint for dressing. Carl hands Anna a brand new carving knife and his wife placed a bowl of hot water on the table. Pulling a flask from his vest Carl told the young soldier to drink as much as possible from it.

Wiping the wound down with hot water Anna could finally see that the bullet was pushing through the skin on the other side of the entrance wound. "I can see the bullet. It's almost broke the skin. I'll do this as quickly as I can." She squeezes Bethel's hand.

Bethel nodded as Anna ran the knife blade through a candle flame and griped the edge of the table. "I'm ready as I can be."

Carl held down Bethel's shoulders and his wife her feet.

"I'll try not to make too much of an ass of myself." She chuckled.

"Don't fret about us now, just do what you have to." Mrs. Cohen said in a motherly tone, making Bethel very homesick.

Anna held the knife close to the bulging skin and mouthed to Carl that he should talk to Tandy.

"You know, if I was a younger man I'd join the cavalry. Oh, I love horses and it seems dashing to think of riding over the fields, sword waving about…."

Anna made a swift cut and popped the bullet out. Bethel jerked on the table then held her head up to see the wound. "Good, now heat up the blade again and hold it on the wound to seal it up, but not all the way."

"Tandy, I've seen this done enough times that I can…"

Bethel laid her head back down. "You are the surgeon today, Madam."

"What can I get for you?" Mrs. Cohen asked as she released the soldier's feet.

"Silk or linen thread and a medium sized needle." Anna replied, glancing at Bethel for approval and she nodded.

"Yes, I do believe I have a small bit of silk thread." Mrs. Cohen then left to find it in the main part of the store. When she returned she gave the items to Anna.

"Do a continuous stitch, Anna. That outta work best." Bethel again grabbed the table edges. Tears ran down her cheek as Anna closed the wound and tied it off. Carl patted Bethel's shoulder.

"We'll fashion you a splint then I'll take you upstairs. Mama, will get you some soup after you rest a bit."

# Chapter Twenty One

The same day that Bethel lay recovering from surgery George Erwin stood over Brandon Neukirk in the cellar of the Sims house. The bullet his sister fired at him had missed his heart and went out past a lung. He grabbed onto George's pant leg.

"Erwin, you piece of shit! That freak sister of yours is gonna be sorry she was born."

George placed a foot on Neukirk's chest near his chin. "I'm a piece of shit? You're a rapist and nothing I ever do will be that bad! You ain't nobody now asshole and your daddy's name don't mean shit to the Yanks."

Breathing hard Brandon laid his head back on the brick floor. "Bethel should have done a better job at killing me, but then she ain't got no business being a soldier and that sickness is going to end!"

He struggled harder under the large boot pinning him down, making George push downer harder. Neukirk pulled his pistol from a holster and pointed it at his captor, but Erwin reached for the barrel and slid the weapon from the weaker man's hand.

"Nice gun." George remarked as he took several rounds from the ammo pouch on Neukirk's belt and loaded the pistol. Worry planted itself on the wounded man's features.

"You have to take me prisoner. I'm an officer!"

Aiming the gun at Neukirk's forehead George snickered. "I don't have to do anything. You should have kept your mouth shut about my sister. I ain't gonna have you ruining something that is none of yer damned concern!"

Brandon looked sick. "You'd kill me just so she can keep playing where she doesn't belong."

Cocking the pistol George shook his head. "No, just cause you're a prick and I don't like ya."

The gun shot brought Jim Esther running down the inside stairs. "Jesus, I thought that son of a bitch was dead!"

"Hell, so did I, but he pulled a weapon on me when I came to drag his carcass outta here." George looked down at Neukirk with disdain. "I took it and shot him with his own gun."

\*\*\*\*\*\*\*\*\*\*\*\*\*\*\*\*\*\*\*\*\*\*

That night Bethel Erwin sat peering out the bedroom window at the Cohen house at the city below. The chicken broth Mrs. Cohen made was delicious and hot as she sipped it from a coffee cup. It reminded Bethel of home, a bitter sweet thing since nothing would ever be the same again. There was a gentle knock at the door and she bade them to enter.

With a clean uniform draped over her arm Anna stepped through the door and laid the clothes on a large trunk. "Good to see you with some color in your cheeks."

Bethel smiled and put the cup down on a quaint little bedside table. "I must have been more tired than I thought, but then we had been without decent food or sleep for months before we joined the Yanks."

Anna pulled a rocking chair up close to the bed. "Not to mention that only an idiot would be cut on without pain medication. You have been asleep for two days and I think we need to have a conversation, Mr. Scott!"

Clearing her throat Bethel pulled herself up in the bed, wincing some from the leg pain. "I know." She looked down at the nightshirt she wore. "Who changed my clothes?"

"I did."

Blushing deeply Bethel studied her hands. "So, there's no doubt now is there? I don't know what to say…you must hate me. I caused you to feel in unnatural ways."

Anna took Bethel's right hand. "I could never hate you, but I do admit that my head and heart and been in a conundrum since we met. I've also never felt more loved and that cannot be an evil thing, Bethel."

"I never meant to hurt anyone…it was an adventure, a duty. Never did I dream that I would care for someone like you. I'm so sorry." Tears filled Bethel's eyes.

Reaching up to touch Bethel's face Anna smiled. "You did a wonderful job with the beard."

"I had a good teacher. I never would have thought of making it, but I met a lady actor in Nashville that put it on for me. She sent me spirit gum ever so often and I used my own hair to patch it." Bethel studied Anna's face and felt a glowing warmness settle over her.

"Was it your brother who was killed then?"

"Yes, Ed. He was George and me's baby brother. He didn't much like being called that though." A shy grin crept onto Bethel's thin lips.

"You're not going back to the Army are you?" Anna asked, though she knew the response.

"I had planned to, at least until I get caught. Had a real close call with that son of a dog Brandon Neukirk, but he won't be a problem anymore."

Anna let out a breath and leaned back in the rocking chair. "I knew there was something special about you. After I was raped, I felt so safe with you. I guess I kind of knew it then, but did not want to face it….."

Scooting closer to the edge of the bed Bethel squeezed Anna's long, thin fingers. Granny would say they were fiddler's hands. "It's all right now, Anna. No one needs to know and no need for you to feel any shame. I'll get on outta here."

Anna shook her head and the locks of her hair fell gently around her shoulders. "No, you don't understand. I love you; I don't want you to walk out of my life."

"George tried to tell me that I was just dreaming that I could never have a life with you." Bethel let the tears roll down her cheeks and Anna put her arms around her.

"What I feel for you I didn't have with Michael. It is a shock to me to find such passion with another woman. You know, you are a very convincing young man. I don't think anyone else knows.'
Bethel held Anna tight then leaned back. "I've known more freedom and respect in the last year that I've ever known. I don't know that I ever want to live as a woman again, Anna."
 Anna looked surprised. "Never again is a long time. How?
"The actor friend I mentioned has been living as a man for the past ten years. If Kim can do it so can I."
"You couldn't go back home to live, so how would your family feel about it?"
 "Well, they all know I'm a duck out of water around there. I think my grandma was trying to tell me something before I left, but I didn't hear her. She told me that I could go through life without a man, so I think she knows me better than I do. Besides, I want to attend medical school and I can't do that wearing a dress. Are you going to stay in Corinth?"
 Anna studied her hands for a moment. Her life in Corinth was over, Michael now part of a distant life where cannon fire and brutalities had only been fodder for late night stories.
"I don't think so. My family lives in the Boston area and I will go back east." She looked at Bethel. "There is a good hospital there where they have clinical studies. You could come with me you could sign up for lectures."
 Bethel laid her head on Anna's shoulder. "I assumed you would be very angry at me fooling you, maybe even give me up. It was wrong of me to let you think I was a man, wrong and selfish."
Anna felt Bethel's soft hair against her cheek. "Do you feel the same about me? I haven't heard you say it?"
 Bethel kissed her for what seemed like an eternity then pulled back. "Yes, I do love you, Anna and I do want to move back east. I also need to finish what I started. I'll understand if you don't want to wait on my foolishness."
Anna felt almost drunk from the kiss. "It's not foolish, but I'll spend every day in worry until you come back to me."
 Bethel smiled and winked at Anna. "I seem to be healing well thanks to a certain nurse. Think I could try walking tomorrow?"
"I well imagine that you will do it anyway, Tandy Scott."

# Chapter Twenty-Two
## August 1862
## North of Corinth


The Union army worked under a blazing sun to repair railroad tracks damaged by retreating Confederate troops. It felt like a blast furnace to those sweltering beneath a merciless sun. George, Jim Esther and Tim have removed their shirts along with numerous Negro men also swinging sledge hammers.

George wiped the sweat from his brow that kept stinging his eyes. "No wonder the Rebs wanted he hell outta here. I sure don't remember it being this damned hot back home."

A small creek flows near the track bed; it is rank and dark colored. Jim Esther screws up his face at the sight. "Rebs are the pissingest, shittingest people I ever seen! The water around here looks like molasses in December."

Tim removed the plug from his canteen and peered into the murkiness. "That's no lie. I boiled this poison for an hour just to kill the smell."

George held the spike while Esther slammed it into the wooden tie then he stood up. "Well, when they come chargin' back this way you can torture a few of them. But just remember that we helped make this city a shit hole."

Grabbing another spike and inserting it into the metal slot, Esther smirked. "Too bad we can't all have them cushy jobs in the hospital like Scott. Hell, I should shoot my own leg!"

"Oh shit, not me. I got no use for bein' around men doin' nothin' but pukin' and shittin' all day long. I had my fill of that, thank you." Tim shook his head.

George slapped his cousin on the shoulder. "I sincerely hope that you never have children, Carter. You got the compassion of a ground squirrel."

The Negro crew laid down several new rails as Esther watched, then belched loudly. "Hell, I'd get shot just so that Anna Harold could take care of me."

Tim winked at George, "I have to admit that she ain't hard to look at. Can't imagine what she sees in old Tandy, the scrawny little shit."

\*\*\*\*\*\*\*\*\*\*\*\*\*\*\*\*\*\*\*\*\*\*\*\*\*

Several months later in October, the surgeon at the hospital in Corinth sat in his office watching a talented young assistant, Tandy Scott care for patients. When Scott looked his way Dr. Taylor Mansfield motioned for the young man to enter his office.

He wanted to keep Scott there, but the shortage of surgeons in the field was critical. Mansfield rubbed his beard as Tandy stood erect in the doorway. "As much as I need you here, Scott, they need you more in the field. Report to Captain Merriweather at Battery Robinette Park in the morning."

"Yes sir, right away. Shall I take supplies Sir?"

Mansfield studied orders on his cluttered desk top. "Pack a bag with extra surgical instruments and take a box of chloroform. They already have a medicine wagon out there. Watch yourself, son."

Bethel took the orders he handed to her and saluted, then spun around and headed for the supply room. She began to fill a bag from the shelves. Anna watched through the open door as she trained nurse volunteers on dressing changes. Her heart began to pound as she studied Bethel's face in the dimly lit storage room.

"Anna, could you come help me please?"

Anna excused herself to the students and crossed the room with a dignified grace, her skirts gliding about her like clouds. "You're going to the front aren't you?"

"Out to Robinette Park, not too far from your homestead." Bethel placed a box of chloroform into the large, black bag.

Anna's voice was strained. "The fighting is bad. You could be overrun."

Bethel took Anna's hand out of sight of the curious volunteers. "Then we'll be treating both sides. I'll be fine, I promise." Looking at the floor, Anna's eyes begin to water. "I'll come back!"

"You can't run the way you used to..."She bit her lip to stop the tears.

"And that's why I am on medical duty now. Don't worry about me; you just take care of our boys here!"

Anna placed bandages into the bag. "I almost wish that I was the one going to the field, the waiting behind the lines is unbearable." She let out a deep sigh. "I've had my moment of weakness and now I shall put on my brave face and tend to these suffering young men."

Bethel kissed her on the check which erupted in giggles from the volunteers. "And you are wonderful at it! I can tell you that you're smile and kind words do as much as our medicines."

A woman's face was a menagerie of characteristics, something that Anna had never noticed before meeting Bethel. Her blue eyes were kind with a mischievous spark, her bone structure displayed strength and faithfulness and the crooked grin had stolen her heart. How would she ever go through life if Bethel died on the battlefield?

## Chapter Twenty-Three

The Union had made use of the old Reb fortifications at Battery Robinette Park as Bethel could see while cresting a hill. They must have left in a hurry or else the Rebs would have destroyed everything to keep the enemy from using it. Funny how a change in uniform could change a person's identity as it was only a short time ago that she was a Confederate soldier.

In the distance Captain Merriweather shouted orders from his horse in preparation of a returning and refreshed Rebel army. She made a few clicks with her tongue and the young dapple trotted toward the officer.

"Private Scott, Sir. Reporting as ordered."

Merriweather reached into a deep pocket and pulled out a handful of patches that he handed to Bethel. "Sew these on when you get a chance, Scott. I need you to have more authority to get things done. The medical insignia goes on the forearm of your sleeve. We're having some trouble finding a clean water source. You wouldn't happen to know of a place we could use for a field hospital?

Visions of Anna's farm before the house burnt made her smile. "Yes, sir. About a mile from here on Turner Creek. The creek water is bad, but there is a homestead there with good well water and a large barn. At least there was a few weeks ago".

The captain shouted at some soldiers not moving fast enough. Merriweather looked older than when she had first seen him at their country church, which seemed like decades ago. "The surgeon, Dr. Keiffer, is waiting just southwest of here. Go find him and tell him where this place is and set up if the water is good. We don't need the barn, but it would be an asset."
"And if the water isn't good?" She asked.

He looked around the fort area for a moment. "Set up anyway. We need a hospital away from here. We can boil the creek water and make do."

Bethel saluted then rode off in the direction of the medicine wagon in the distance. Glancing at the patches in her hand she found that they indicated the rank of Sergeant Major. She was both surprised and pleased with the promotion and peered back at Merriweather, but he had already ridden off in another direction. The medicine wagon and two ambulances ambled along a deeply rutted road framed by barren fields on both sides. One of the ambulances was a four wheel type, but the other made Bethel cuss out loud. Two wheelers probably killed as many patients as bullets and the trots.

As the new Sergeant Major rode up, a bleary eyed Dr. Keiffer looked up from the horses' rumps he had been staring at while trying not to fall asleep. Bethel saluted and the older man just waved his hand at her. He was about forty with hair that was either gray or covered in dust. "No need of that with me." The doctor coughed.
"I'm Sergeant Major Scott. Captain Merriweather sent me to find you and take you to a new hospital location near here." She pulled her cap down further against the cold wind.
"That a fact? What is your specialty, Sgt. Scott?" He asked peering over dirty glasses. At that time two litter carriers came around from the other side of the wagon to take a look at her.
"I've been working as an assistant surgeon, Doctor. "
"Well, that I can use. I do hope this new location has some attributes that led aid to the care of patients!" Keiffer replied with an air of sarcasm.

**\*\*\*\*\*\*\*\*\*\*\*\*\*\*\*\*\*\*\*\*\*\*\*\***

That evening the four of them picked through the burned out remains of Anna's house to find anything that might be of use. The well water was still good and it did not appear that any troops had been through the property. The creek then was polluted from camps upstream. The barn still stood vigil over the land, much to the doctor's delight.

At dawn they began setting up the hospital by removing the doors from the house for use as operating tables and beds for the more severely wounded inside the barn. Those less injured would either lie in the open or in tents soon coming. To Bethel's pleasure, the two litter carriers were, in fact, very efficient and could perform basic patient care.

When the rest of the supplies came two days later, so did the wounded. The interior of the barn was lit up by lanterns with a third surgeon helping with the amputations. Emery Morgan had been an army doctor before the war, providing Bethel with a wealth of information and he was interested in her home remedies as well. She looked over a wagon load of bloody soldiers with two privates waiting for instructions.

"Take this one and this one over to the surgeons. Lay the other three to the side, they can wait awhile." The two privates immediately obeyed the order.

Piles of amputated limbs lie near the operating tables in the barn. The lantern light was too dim, but some patients cannot wait until daybreak for treatment. Bethel scanned the area for an unoccupied soldier. When she saw one, Bethel ordered him to dig a hole for the mountains of body parts beginning to get in the way. The private pissed and moaned that such duty was all he had seen in the war.

"At least you still got your arms and legs! She shouted in irritation and fatigue.

As the sun came up, the wounded had slowed to a trickle. Keiffer finished up some stitching and nodded to a wagon pulling up with more wounded.

"I got this if you want to go survey the new crop."

Bethel nodded with her eyes bloodshot from lack of sleep. She hurried over to the wagon in the chilly morning air to find men piled on top on each other. "Jesus, I wish they wouldn't do that!" She thought for a moment that the ones on the bottom should be warm enough then said aloud to a corporal having coffee. "Carl! Come give me a hand here."

She climbed up into the wagon bed, prompting groans and pleas for water from the injured. "You're all gonna be just fine now. Take these two and put 'em under that big oak, we're full up in the barn."

Carl motioned for a private to bring a stretcher over and they move the men on top. On the bottom Bethel saw a soldier whose face was full of blood and she placed two fingers on his carotid to check for a pulse. The man grabbed her arm suddenly, startling Bethel.

"Beth, help me." It was Tim. His voice was very weak.

She held his hand while peering back to see if anyone had heard him say her name. Bethel whispered, "I'll help ya, but if you say that name again I'll kick yer ass!" Tim squeezed her hand and grinned slightly. "This man is next! Get me a stretcher now!"

Dr. Morgan examined the bullet wound under Tim's left eye. He stuck a finger in to feel for the slug. "I fear the bullet has gone into the sinus cavity and from there to where?"

Blood drained from Tim's ears and nose. Bethel shouted at him. "Tim, you ain't leaving us now. All you've seen is a few baby elephants!" Her voice trailed off as his pupils dilated and his head rolled off to the side, blood pouring from his mouth.

"I'm sorry, Scott. It's hard losing friends like this." Morgan gripped Bethel's shoulder.

The clatter and jingling of ambulances returning from the hospital in town pulled their attention outside the barn. A corporal jumped down from the lead wagon with a paper in his hand. He approached the barn and saluted.

"Got a message here from Colonel Baldwin for a Sgt. Major Scott."

"Doesn't seem like he should be referring to me." She said to Dr. Morgan, trying to keep control of her emotions.

"That's army life, Scott, just one opportunity for advancement after another." The doctor replied as he motioned for a litter bearer to move Tim outside for burial.

Bethel reluctantly stepped away from her recently deceased cousin and took the missive from the young corporal. It was short and to the point, military style. The Rebs had retreated and she was to return to the division hospital in Corinth.

"Looks like I'm going back to the big city. Johnny has turn tail and run." Bethel said as she stopped the men carrying Tim and removed a letter to his mother from a breast pocket. The warm blood from his mouth sent steamy clouds into the frigid air.

Peering over blood smeared glasses Morgan shook his head. "Damn, it was good to finally have adequate staff for a change!" She nodded that it was okay to take Tim away. It was so odd how one second a person could be talking to you and in the next be gone with only a borrowed husk remaining. Bethel was glad that she had not seen the corpse of her little brother. Life and death had began to merge for her and she was not sure how she would ever return to a normal life again, assuming that she lived through the war.

"When are you supposed to report for duty?" Dr. Morgan stepped out of the barn, wiping his bloody hands with a rag.

"Tomorrow morning." She replied as a light mist began to fall. It would turn to snow soon.

"Have some dinner and then grab some shut eye. You need it, son. Climb up there in loft where you won't be bothered. " Morgan smiled then headed for the mess area.

The cook had moved the stove from Anna's kitchen out into the yard where he had baked some corn bread and fried up venison from a deer shot by one of the privates. Bethel grinned at the ingenuity, especially since Anna would appreciate the thriftiness and so would her mother, Jane Erwin. After eating her fill, sleep overcame her and Bethel made her way to the loft where she slept solid until dawn.

## Chapter Twenty-Three
Corinth
October 1862


There was a shortage of beds at the division hospital in Corinth and some patients were lying on the floor as Bethel walked through the front doors onto the ward. The chief surgeon, Dr. Taylor Mansfield, was discussing patient treatment with Anna at the far end of the ward. The sight of all those patients took the spirit out of Bethel. Was this nightmare ever going to end?

Mansfield excused himself and approached his assistant surgeon. "I heard about your cousin, Tim, and I'm very sorry. Go wash up and get some breakfast in the kitchen. You look exhausted. I wish I could give you a furlough, but as you can see we're swamped."

"I'm fine. I shouldn't be, but I am. I will take something to eat though."

The doctor was concerned with the young man's bloodshot eyes and thin appearance, but there was little that could be done about it. Scott looked like everybody else. "Go on, Scott, and congratulations on your promotion, now I can delegate even more chores for you!"

With a casual salute Bethel turned and headed out of the ward and down the hall to the left to the kitchen. The hospital had once been a hotel that the army requisitioned with a good supply of pots and pans and a large stove. Breakfast had just been served to the patients and a volunteer nurse was busy scrubbing dishes. Bethel sat down at a long white table with plates and glasses stacked in the middle.

"I'll be right with ya, sir." Missy O'Reilly shook soap off her hands and grabbed a dish towel.

"Don't go to any trouble for me, please. I can always eat later." Bethel felt badly that the woman was going to dirty anything else up for her.

Anna Harold came through the kitchen door. "I'll finish those, Missy. Get yourself a little fresh air and then make another round on the second ward."

"Oh thank the Lord! My hands are redder than lobster claws! Sgt. Scott we got some scrambled eggs and toast left. I put it on a plate there on the stove to stay warm."

Bethel removed her hat and placed on a chair beside her. "Please just call me Tandy when no one from the army is around."

Wiping her hands dry, Missy smiled at Anna who stood next to Bethel. "I appreciate that. I'm not much into all this military discipline, though Anna here runs this place like a ship's captain."

Anna blushed slightly. "Oh I do not!"

After Missy cheerfully leaned against the back door as Bethel removed the wool uniform blouse in the too warm kitchen. She wore a blue and white gingham shirt and brown suspenders. "Yes, I can believe you do! But these boys here are surviving to go home or back to the front because of you nurses, so I have no complaints."

"I wish you were the surgeon then, Tandy. Well, I'll step out for a quick moment then get back to the ward, Anna." Missy disappeared through the door with a wave.

Anna went over to the large stove and fetched the plate of eggs. She brought over to the table as Bethel pulled patches from the blouse pocket.

"They gave me these, but I can't sew worth a damn." Bethel shrugged her shoulders.

Anna sat down across from Bethel with a slight grin on her lips. "Now that's funny coming from an assistant surgeon."

Bethel bit her lip as she forked a wad of scrambled eggs. "I had not thought of it that way." She laughed.

"I can do it for you. Let me get you some butter for that toast...."

Bethel grabbed her hand. "No, I don't need any. Just sit for a minute. Yesterday when I saw Tim die it was made clear to me that I might not make it through the war. I've seen hundreds of people die before, but this time it was different, too close to home."

"To me every day is too close. As long as you wear that uniform your future is in jeopardy." Anna squeezed Bethel's hand.

"I have a pension coming whether I make it or not. I want you to have it if I don't." Bethel studied Anna's face for comprehension.

"What are saying?" Anna asked, not knowing what Bethel was thinking.

"Marry me."

Anna sat back in the chair, completely stunned.

"I'm not asking for eternity, only that you are taken care of if I'm killed."

Anna leaned into the table. "It isn't the idea of spending eternity with you takes  my words from me. It is the fact that I want to say yes."

Bethel smiled broadly. "Then let's do it before I get sent somewhere else." She looked around to see if anyone was listening in, but the kitchen was empty except for the two of them. "Besides, it will help me to be a married 'man' and you will be safer as a married woman." Anna looked at her so sweetly that Bethel wanted to run off with her at that moment. "I really want to marry you because I love you and I want to" Bethel's voice had softened.

" I accept your proposal, Tandy Scott." Anna smiled. "Now eat those eggs before they cool off! They're not easy to come by you know." She got up from the table and came around to Bethel's side and kissed her on the lips before going back to the wards.

\*\*\*\*\*\*\*\*\*\*\*\*\*\*\*\*\*\*\*\*\*\*

A week later at the First Methodist Church, Bethel and Anna waited in line with dozens of other soldiers and their future brides. War was dangerous and painful, but Bethel had to admit that at times there was a romantic side to it, and people seemed to appreciate what they possessed and could lose at anytime. Falling in love with a soldier was exciting and many were marrying in case there was no tomorrow. For many there would not be.

When their names were called the two of them stood up and walked down the aisle to where the preacher waited before a podium. George stood up for Bethel and Billie Jean was the Maid of Honor. She giggled and peered at George behind the couple, making him blush.

The medium sized church was packed with other couples waiting to tie the knot. Bethel was nervous and felt like she needed to swallow, but could not. Anna reached for her hand and squeezed it. The experience was more familiar to Anna with the young army sergeant being her second "husband". With a pounding heart Bethel struggled to hear the preacher's words over the coughing and shuffling about of people in the crowded pews. Reverend Subrin was direct and quick. Bethel heard the words "I do" escape from her mouth.

"I now pronounce you husband and wife. You may kiss the bride." Subrin, nodded and smiled. With square shaped gold glasses and tuffs of gray hair sticking out everywhere he looked like an elf. George watched his beaming sister lift Anna's veil and kiss her. He had never seen her face brighten in such a manner. Glancing at Billie Jean, George wondered if she felt the same about him as he was pretty sure he was in love with her.

"Next! I have a lot of weddings today!" Subrin announced cheerfully while accepting the two dollars Bethel have him. The four of them turned and ran down the aisle to the roar and clapping of other soldiers and their sweethearts. Once outside the church George shakes his head and chuckles at Bethel.

"Didn't think I'd ever marry did ya?" She nudged him with her elbow.

"No, but then nothing you do anymore surprises me. Too bad we don't have time for a party cause we could sure use one. I got get back to camp, only got a two hour pass. I'll be damned, Tandy is a married man!" He grabbed his sister, pulled her aside and whispered. "You owe me, ya little shit. Ma and Pa will have a cow."

"Only if you tell 'em." Bethel stated as a matter of fact.

Anna and Billie Jean laughed at the interaction of the two soldiers. Billie does not know that Tandy Scott is a woman and squeezed her sister's arm in playfulness.

"What did he say?" She asked Bethel.

"Ah, just man talk. Never you mind now." George grinned.

"If only we could get on a train and go far away from here and this war. But we have a hospital full of wounded or sick men." Anna put her arms around Bethel.

One side of Bethel's mouth curled up in a crooked grin and she pulled Anna to her. For the first time in her life Bethel was truly happy. She could now express her love for another woman without anyone giving her more than a passing glance. When she saw George batting his eyes at her and sighing Bethel remarked, "No it's your turn, Mr. Erwin."

Billie wore a white print dress covered with tiny red flowers. She moved back and forth making her skirt sway, smiling sweetly at George.

"Duty calls people, and though I dread to leave suddenly, I must!" George walked backwards with his hands clasped behind his back.

The other men in George's company were gathering for the march back to camp. Not all of the soldiers waiting to get hitched would have the chance that day. Some would get a second chance at matrimony and others would either face the surgeon or be rolled into an open trench in the field. Bethel tried to block out the reality in order to enjoy her own happiness, but it was difficult. Anna kissed her cheek as if the dour thoughts had leaked into the cold air.

"Take care, George and we'll see you soon." Bethel hollered at her brother.

# Chapter Twenty-four
Eastern Tennessee
December 1862


A few miles east of Longmire, Union troops worked to repair damage done to two railroad bridges.  Troops guarded the bridge while the rails were replaced. Bill Erwin took in the scene from a wooded hill overlooking the bridges. The trees in the distance are bathed in low lying clouds and the river below covered with ice except for a thin stream still fighting the freezing air.
Erwin's main focus was on two Rebels nearby. One had a pair of binoculars and the other a rifle. Both were young, gaunt and out to stop the Yanks from fixing a line of transportation. Bill shot the boy with the rifle when he aimed it at the troops on the bridge. The lookout moved to grab the pistol from his belt.
"Don't!" Erwin commanded.
In a few quick strides over to the frightened Reb, Bill jerked the gun away from him, shoving the pistol under his own belt. He signaled the troops on the bridge with a small mirror. "Get yer ass up and walk ten paces ahead of me!"

The lookout got to his feet after slipping and falling on his tail bone several times. Bill rolled his eyes like a disgusted parent. "Take yer time, boy, but stand up!" The slouch that hid the boy's eyes, but Erwin could see tears running through the dirt on his face. He wore a tattered Confederate uniform shirt with clothes he had previously worn to farm. In a moment of humiliation he shouted at his captor.

"You treacherous son of a whore! You outta be ashamed of yerself..."

Bill slapped the boy across the back of his head. The hat flew off and rolled down the snow covered hill.

"Goddamn it old man. That was my only hat!" The kid wiped the tears off with his sleeve.

"Shoulda gave that some thought before you degraded my poor dead mother." Bill smirked and nodded toward the rugged trail down the hill. "Now move."

He took the prisoner to a wall tent set up near the bridge with a chimney at one end from where smoked rolled up lazily into the gray sky. A soldier stood guard outside the command tent and he dropped the rifle from his shoulder to a defense position.

"You must be new. I'm Bill Erwin and this skunk was fixin' to plunk down a few of yer boys."

The tent flaps parted as Major Porter emerged from inside. He bore an enormous blonde handle bar mustache and towered over the other two men. "I don't know which is scarier, you or that scoundrel with ya!"

"The other one ain't in this world anymore." Bill frowned at the lookout who glanced sideways at him.

Porter took a handful of the boy's brown hair. "Well, this little varmint is gonna talk to me or wish he'd caught the same train!" He motioned for two soldiers near the bridge to approach. "Get this critter back to camp. Don't put him with the other prisoners until we interrogate him.

Bill watched as the two soldiers poked and prodded the young man along the road. "I should get on home before it gets dark."

"You've earned a night by the fire old man!" Porter chuckled as his disappeared through the tent flaps.

Esther waited until the major went back into the tent and then spoke to Erwin. "I knew an Erwin when I was with the 58th Illinois in Corinth. Name was George and he had two cousins with him, Tandy and Tim."

"They're my kin. God, it's been so long since I've seen them." Bill smiled at hearing their names.

"I really liked them. I'll tell ya though, that Tandy married the best looking woman in the state! Damned near all the boys wanted to trade him places."

Erwin's expression changed slightly as he processed the information. Esther kept talking. "It wasn't a bit fair neither that George got the sister. Keep it in the family, huh! Hey, I'm real sorry about Tim. He was a good friend."

"What you say your name is? I'd like to tell 'em I ran into ya when we write again."

"Jim Esther."

"Well, Tandy is at the hospital in Mound City and George is guarding prisoners at Cairo. Wish I could have seen that wedding….in a church and all was it?" Bill prodded for information.

"Yes, weren't nothing fancy. This one minister picks a Saturday and does nothing but weddings. Anna lost everything in a fire and so she made a pretty dress just for the occasion. They sure made a handsome couple." Jim looked to the clouds as if an image of the event floated up there.

"Tandy married someone named Anna then, and George was there too?"

"Hell, he was the best man. Didn't they write home about it?" Esther pulled his attention back to Bill.

"The mail ain't always so reliable around here. I'm sure we're missin' a few letters." A gust of cold wind made Bill pull his hat further down his forehead.

Jim stepped back into his post outside the command tent. "Mighty proud to meet ya. You tell 'em that I asked after 'em."

Bill nodded. "I'll do that. You take care now, son."

On the long walk home it began to spit snow. The wind was icy and the thick clouds made it seem later. The trees were black, barren streaks against a gray canvas. Bill had never been that religious and had hardly read any of the Bible. He left it up to his wife to steer the family in the right direction. However, he was disturbed by Bethel's behavior. It was no secret that she was a little odd for a girl and Bill never expected her to have a bunch of kids, but neither had he ever dreamed that she would join the army and marry a woman. How the hell was Jane going to take that bit of news?

# Chapter Twenty-five
Mound City, Illinois

By Christmas Eve, 1863 Bethel has been promoted to lieutenant. She makes rounds in a ward at the General Hospital wearing an officer's blue frock coat.  The nurses and nuns have made decorations out of every little bit of scrap material that could be found.  Checking each patient, Bethel appears solemn.

From a barrel in the corner Anna pours cups of apple cider for the patients. The apples had been picked from a nearby orchard that fall. George emerged from a back room carrying an old banjo and placed a hand on Anna's shoulder. He was on a short furlough from the POW camp at Cairo.

After a quick wink at Anna, George began to strum the banjo, making Bethel turn around.  Patients able to move raise their heads to see who is playing. In a deep baritone he started singing an old Christmas song from back home, What Are You Gonna Call That Pretty Little Baby?

"The Virgin Mary had one son, oh, oh, glory Hallelujah...." As he strolled through the ward he beckoned in sister to join him. Bethel shook her head that she would not and George nodded in the affirmative. "Glory be to the new born king!"

Bethel looked away with a grin on her face and laughed when George poked her in the ribs with the banjo neck. George keeps singing as she looks down on a young man with an amputated leg. He smiles for the first time since being admitted.

"Mary, what are you gonna call that pretty little baby?" George sings as deep as he can.

"Some call him David; I think I'll call him Emmanuel." Bethel responded in a clear voice that passed for tenor.

They then sang together as Anna swirled around in her maroon dress as a nun carried the cider on a large tray. Anna served the delighted men then danced to the next patient. The patients able to clap and sing along did so, which made the nuns in the kitchen emerge with dish clothes in hand. They were amused to see the assistant surgeon so light hearted and the patients happy.

George wandered from bed to bed singing loudly. Bethel took Anna's hands and waltzed her down the aisle toward the giggling nuns who knew the song and joined in. The finale came when George dropped to his knees, strumming the strings with gusto. He stood up and bowed to the cheering patients all around him.

Bethel hugged Anna then walked up to her brother. "Thank you, Sgt. Erwin for that lapse into lunacy. Now get before the surgeon kills me!"

He grinned mischievously and leaned into close to her while pulling a letter from his pocket. "He'll have to get in line. It's from Pa. I didn't open it, but I well imagine that he wants to know all about your new bride."

Bethel looks puzzled. She yanks George into her office. "Just how did he find out about that?"

"Jim Esther transferred to engineers and they're working close to home."

She plopped down behind the old wood desk and let a sigh. "Shit, I never counted on this happening. Damn it."

"Well, I don't know what his letter to you says, but in mine he says that he had a talk with grandma and she says folks have to be true to their own natures, even if contrary to common thought. Ma's in a state of shock though." George grinned like a Cheshire cat. Bethel looked distressed. "You didn't think you could hide forever did ya?" She slowly stood up. "I had not planned that far ahead."

Anna knocked then leaned through the door. "You're not discussing secret plots are you?

"No, but Tandy could use the skills of a Pinkerton man about now. I need to get back. Some of the fellas are putting on a Christmas play and I promised to play a wise man." George snickers as he goes through the door.


"That should be one hell of an acting job!" Bethel retorts.

Setting the banjo down in the corner, George tips his hat. "Merry Christmas, Anna."

"I know I'm missing something here. Do I even want to know what it is?" Anna looks back and forth between them.

"We'll talk about it later. Why don't we check the patients one more time then we'll leave it to the sisters." Bethel kissed Anna's cheek. An hour later as they strolled though the camp covered with a blanket of snow they could hear men singing in the distance. The married officer's quarters consisted of several rows of small wood buildings. Anna took Bethel's arm as they walk back to their quarters.

"Want to tell me what George gave you before we get home?" Snow fell in huge flakes as Bethel shook her head. "It's Christmas Eve, Anna. Let's not ruin it. Look how pretty it is out here…snow can even improve an army post."

Anna stopped. "You will be distracted the rest of the night, so just tell me what it is."

Reaching into an inside pocket Bethel retrieved her father's letter. She had read it while mixing drugs for a patient with a fierce infection. "My parents are very good people, but they also kept poking me to find a husband. I knew that wasn't going to happen. I don't need to be told about how I'm going to hell…They found out that I married another woman." Bethel lowered her voice though they were alone on the road.

"They are pretty religious then?"

"Yes and no. They're not fanatics, but they are simple mountain folk. So am I, but I have also had to look at life differently because I am different. Grandma understands that and George says she took up for me."

Anna took the letter and stuck back into Bethel's pocket. "We have not done anything to be sent to hell for, now have we? What you have done is given me a better life than I would have had as a widow with a child and my presence has made your life easier as a soldier."

Bethel studied the snowflakes accumulating on her boots and considered the truth in what Anna said. Once they had been transferred to Mound City, Anna had sent for her daughter, Ella. There were other children at the post and she could bear being without the child no longer. Bethel couldn't say no, but did have reservations about having a small child with them.

Physically, they had indeed done nothing to court the devil beyond kissing and cuddling. It scared the hell right out of Bethel who had no experience with sexual relations. She had experienced many crushes back home, but did not dare let anyone know how she felt, much less attempt to do something about it. When Anna slipped her arms around her and went to sleep on her "husband's" shoulder it made Bethel's heart pound against her sternum.

"You always manage to make me sound so noble." The young officer replied.

Anna continued walking, pulling her partner along with her. "That is because you are my best friend and you are mine!" Walk with me to pick up Ella. I think Billie Jean would like to see George in the play without the distraction."

"It isn't right that the women who do our laundry, sew for us, write letters for the disabled, do not have their service recognized. Billie works so hard washing uniforms..."

Anna shook her head and put a finger to her lips. "It's Christmas Eve, sweetheart. Let's not think of the war or the many imperfections of society. Besides, Billie Jean enjoys the laundry business she has with the other ladies and it is no small advantage that she gets to be close to George either!"

"She had me worried for awhile after you told her about me. Her reaction was so...."

"Hostile? Dramatic? That's just Billie Jean in the most normal of daily life. We did throw quite a bit at her all at once. I knew she would eventually follow us after a month of living with jus the Cohens."

The couple approached a small cabin with a tripod in front holding a large kettle. A lantern inside casts silhouettes against the curtains of those moving around. A shorter shape jumping up and down indicates that little Ella is still awake.

Bethel turned to Anna. "The night air isn't too chilly tonight, why don't we bundle Ella up and we all go to the play?"

The flames of the cook fire dance in Anna's eyes. "That is a fine idea Lt. Scott. Is that an order?"

"Why yes it is. I just believe that is the thing to do this snowy evening."

*****************************

January 15, 1864

For most of the afternoon Anna had sat in their cabin mending socks and sewing on uniform buttons. Ella played with wooden toys one of the soldiers had carved for her near the small fireplace. The air was frigid and it made handing a needle cumbersome as her fingers were numb. The little girl laughed as she moved the wooden train around, her breath creating white clouds that hovered inside.

There were footsteps outside and then Bethel appeared through the door. She did not look happy and failed to hide it.

"You're going to tell me something I don't want to hear?" Anna laid the sock on a stool next to her chair.

Removing her hat, Bethel sat on a make shift bed of wood crates and a straw mattress. "I don't wish to say it either, but I guess things couldn't go this well for long. We're being shipped out to Vicksburg."

"Can't we just go with you?" Anna asked, knowing the answer.

"No, moving from one bloody fight to another is no life for you and Ella. If you'd like to be closer to us I can arrange for you to work at Cumberland Hospital in Nashville." She smiled at the child who was staring at her.

"You got ice hanging off your mustache!" Ella giggled, her cheeks turning even pinker as she laughed.

Bethel felt along the edges of the mustache and pulled the ice off the tips.

"I haven't been away from you. I doubt very much I will care for it either. As long as we can work together the war is bearable. Billie Jean will follow the company and I could too."

Anna wore a shawl embroidered with bright flowers over a dark pink dress. The soft light of the lantern made Anna appear younger. Bethel knelt down next to her.

"When you look at me like that I lose all resolve to resist. But listen; this time we're going to be in hot, humid places where disease is killing more troops than bullets. I would feel so much better if you were far from it."

Ella shouted out train noises as Anna watched her. "For her sake alone, if it were just me I would not leave you."

Bethel held her hand gently. "This war can't last much longer and then we'll have some decisions to make. I'll have my friend Miles check on you in Nashville. I feel better already."

Gazing sweetly at the kneeling officer next to her, Anna kissed Bethel and then grabbed the socks with holes in the toes. "It's settled then. Now if you don't mind, sir, I have work to do for the army!"

# Chapter Twenty-six
## Pleasant Hill, Louisiana
### April 1864

The Old Stage Road ran through dense forest between Mansfield and Pleasant Hill. The Union was attacked while strung out along the narrow road and they have fallen back. Several brigades were camped on a plateau north and east of the town of Pleasant Hill leaving wide gaps between the brigades that were vulnerable to Reb attacks.

A field hospital was set up a few miles outside of Pleasant Hill. It is humid and many of the northern troops are not acclimated to the heat. Bethel is not suffering as much as some since Tennessee can be just as sultry. She stripped down to a shirt and leather apron smeared with blood. Sweat has saturated her hair and the flies are maddening. Bethel is short and blunt with the orderlies, which is unlike her.

A couple of litter carriers drop a patient roughly to the ground and take off. Bethel yelled at them, "Why don't you worthless son of a bitches just desert!"

Captain Merriweather rode up close to the treatment area where Bethel operated in a tent with the sides rolled up. "Lt. Scott, are you having a problem?" He removed his hat to wipe off the sweat from his forehead.

"Yes sir, I am! I know you got to have seasoned vets on the front lines, but sir, I need some good help here too."

"You're not happy with the litter bearers?" The captain asked as he watched the grimacing patient who had just been dropped.

Bethel knelt down to check his wounds. "No sir, not when every lop-eared jackass is recruited for the job. It would be nice if some of these men could live to go home!" The two orderlies observed nervously from outside the tent where two dozen men waited for treatment.

"I see your point, Lt. I will take care of it. Carry on."

Turning his horse around, the captain glared at the two litter carriers to relay the message of their poor job performance. He continued with the inspection of the hospital and infirmary area, the horse's tail swinging to and fro chasing off flies.

One of the orderlies approached the assistant surgeon fairly sure he was in the lop-eared jackass category. "Lt. who do you want next?"

Bethel emerged from the surgical tent to examine the rows of wounded lying on stretchers. She spends seconds with each patient then barks orders on how to arrange them. "I'm only doing amputations today, how many times do I have to say it? Put this one on the table next."

While the orderlies carry the slight soldier into the tent and place him on the long wooden surgical table, Bethel pours chloroform onto a rag. Standing at the head of the table she finds herself looking down into the face of a woman soldier whose eyes were fixed in terror.

"You'll be fine, just breathe deep now."

The woman grabbed Bethel's arm with a knowing look that they were two of a kind. "Name's Fonda, we got lost in the woods...don't take my leg, please!"

"If I don't you'll die."

"No, hospital! I can't go to the hospital." Fonda pleaded as one of the orderlies stepped up to assist.

Bethel placed the cloth over the patient's mouth and nose. When she passed out the orderly replaced the assistant surgeon at the head of the table and held the patient's arms down.

The orderly shakes his head. "No offense intended, sir, but I don't blame him at all."

Bethel ripped the right pant leg and cut it off above the knee. The leg is shattered near the ankle, so she decided to amputate just below the knee. "And why is that, Private?"

The orderly immediately wished he had not made the comment as Bethel's tone is humorless. The second orderly held the patients feet and answered the question.

"Some of you doctors are real good, sir, but a right fair amount of ya aren't. Being sent to a hospital means a coffin to most of us." Fonda thrashes about as Bethel clamped a tourniquet on the thigh and tightened it down. Taking a scalpel from the tray, she cut through the skin and muscle, and then placed a piece of cloth with two slits in it over the incision to retract the tissue away from the bone. She placed a bow saw on the exposed long bone and sliced through it. When the cloth was removed Bethel could easily see the arteries and veins. The patient struggled to the horror of those waiting, but Bethel did not have time to explain the facts of battlefield medicine and the levels of sedation.

As she sutured the stump Bethel addressed the orderly. "I can promise you soldier that many less of you would be returning home if not for army surgeons. This one goes to New Orleans." She went over to a rain barrel and washed the blood from her hand and arms. Bethel felt for Fonda and knew that dying was not what she feared at the hospital, but exposure.

# Chapter Twenty-seven
Alexandria, Virginia
April 29, 1864

The 2nd Division hospital in Alexandria, Virginia was a sprawling complex of buildings with the wards radiating off the main compound. It housed 993 patients. Most of the patients had been transported by land as the Confederates had blocked river traffic to the Mississippi river.

Bethel was restocking a medicine wagon when two medical cadets smoking pipes wander over. Both are around twenty years old.

"I feel for the patients you shipped out of here to New Orleans. A land trip probably ruined their chances." She stated.

Cadet Kelly, like his buddy, still bore the freshness of someone who could afford ideals. "It was a mess, Lt. We put some really sick boys on those wagons. Goddamn Rebs don't know when to quit."

"Have you seen much action, sir? We have not been in the field as yet." The other cadet, Battin, inquired cautiously as some battle veterans would damned near take your head off for asking.

"We volunteered because we figured we'd get a chance to study with real patients and cadavers are really hard to find in medical school." Kelly interjected as if to qualify the question.

Bethel snorted and the two cadets looked at each other. "I can't imagine cadavers every being in short supply. You get in the field and it won't be long that you'll wish you never saw the inside of a human body."

"We'd love that, sir. I pray we get our chance soon. I really think a person learns better by doing." Battin's enthusiasm was characteristic of his youth.

Bethel closed up the back of the wagon and kicked an empty crate up to the building. "Enjoy your time here, gentlemen. And don't pray too hard, you might get your prayers answered."

She entered the hospital with a list of supplies taken for the field. The leg wound was still bothering Bethel and she walked with a slight limp. Dr. Morton, a middle-aged surgeon emerged from an office with patient charts. He raised an eyebrow at the assistant surgeon's limp.

"Lieutenant, should you be one of our patients?" He inquired over round spectacles.

"Oh no, Doctor. We just had one hell of a march from Louisiana and it's acting up a bit." Bethel stifled responses to the shooting pains coming from around the knee joint.

"I see. What outfit are you with?"

"The 58th Illinois Infantry. I'm Lt. Tandy Scott, assistant surgeon." Bethel removed her hat and stuck it under her arm.

"Oh yes, I've heard good things about you, son. There's some that think you ought to find yourself a medical school when this is all over." Morton grunted. "Assuming it ever will be."

The fact that the surgeon had heard of her surprised Bethel. "I've had good and bad said to me and about me, doctor. Glad that you heard something positive anyway. I'd like to attend medical school."

Morton studied the way she was standing, rubbing his salt and pepper beard. "I don't know that you ought to be in the field with a limp like that. Where are you from?"

"Eastern Tennessee. I don't want a discharge." She fought the anxiety rising in her chest.

"And I am not offering you one, Lieutenant. We have eleven hospitals in Nashville and you could finish your time there. We never have enough decent assistant surgeons."   Morton wrote down the information Bethel gave him.

"My wife is a nurse at the Cumberland. It sure would be a comfort to be near her and closer to home." Bethel felt a surge of relief at the good luck. She watched as Morton walked back into his office and fetched a notepad.

"Oh, you'll still work your ass off. You just won't be getting shot at while doing it, which is some compensation in itself. Write your name and information down here for me and I'll arrange it."

**************************

On December 9, 1864 a freezing rain pummeled Nashville. Army tents were pitched throughout the city and cannons were placed on the steps of the capitol building. It was nearly impossible to walk with soldiers and civilians sliding and falling in the slippery streets.

The bridges over the Cumberland River were fortified by the Union as well as the hills west of Nashville. The Confederate army was strung out between the Granny White and the Hillsborough Turnpikes. The 58th Illinois had been in Nashville since November. George Erwin stood in a bunker on the interior Union line watching the western horizon through spy glasses. With him is Sgt. Cole, an older man whose knees were causing him nothing but pain and trouble in the wet weather. The view is gray and cloudy, but the Rebs can be heard in the distance.

"I can't see a damned thing. Wonder what the hell is going on over there?" George put the glasses down and rubbed his gloved hands together. His words hanging in the air like icicles.

Cole stamped his feet and sat down on an old oak stump. "Probably digging caves to get outta this god forsaken ice!"

"Guess we should be a little grateful we got a roof over our heads. I spent many a night in the rain, snow and ice with nothing blocking me from the elements." George replied, not really feeling all that thankful.

Cole let out a loud moan as he pulled off his right boot. He rubbed the heel of his foot where a large blister was draining. "How much longer can this damned war last?"

## Chapter Twenty-Eight
Cumberland Hospital

Nearly a week later Anna threw bloody rags into a pot bellied stove to destroy them and then threw another log on top of the pile. A volunteer nurse named Martha Withers let in a blast of cold air as she entered the main ward. She was around twenty years old with a slight build and a lingering Irish accent. The young woman was heavily bundled against the icy weather.

"Martha! What are you doing here? It's very treacherous out there." Anna closed the door to the stove, the fire roaring from the added fuel.

"Wasn't easy, ya need a pair of ice skates to move at all, but some places is slushy enough. I seen yer husband over at Number One ripping some poor steward apart. I'm sure glad he seems to like me! Martha removed her heavy, wool outer coat and hung it on a wood rack a few feet from the stove.

"You have common sense, Martha and much of the healing arts is just that. But why on earth did you venture over here instead of going home?"

"Lt. Scott said you might be short handed, so I come to see for sure." Martha pulled off her gloves and held her hands over the stove top.

"Tandy sent you out in this mess?" Anna asked with surprise.

"Oh no, he told me to get on home, but I live close by. It was just as easy to come here." Martha shrugged. In truth, her husband was most likely drunk and the place cluttered from his laying about all day.

"You're a saint, Martha. The poor nuns are being worked to death, but they are immune to so much that they can just keep going." Anna glanced around the ward at the Sisters of Mercy who tended patients.

"They're used to taking orders too, something I've got a bit of a problem with! You ought to be getting home to the little one." Martha pointed a finger toward Anna.

As Anna walked through the ward with Martha in tow they observe the patients and note their condition. The ward was just one at Cumberland Hospital which housed nine hundred beds.

"The weather is taking its usual toll I'm afraid. The patients are already weak from wounds and malnutrition and have little left to fight disease. The best we can do for them is to keep them clean and hydrated." Anna smiled at one of the nuns changing a bandage.

Martha leaned close to Anna. "I learned from your husband not to give the ones with the trots Epson salts, but Captain Sanders makes us do it. Thank Jesus and Mary he's not working tonight!"

A patient with his arm in a sling sitting on the edge of his bed over heard Martha and snickered. Bethel strolled over to the dark haired youth and winked. "That's what I like to see, my patients laughing!"

"Anna, why don't you go on home and I will be along shortly. I just want to catch up on paperwork before leaving tonight." Bethel points toward her office.

T  he idea displeased Anna, but she knew that the work needed to be done or it piled up very easily. "I will get a fire going and warm up some soup. Don't take too long!"

A       n hour later Bethel emerged from General Hospital Number One onto the dark street. The night was quiet except for the muffled sounds of troops in tents a block away. She stepped cautiously into the icy street.

In one of the tents four soldiers and a civilian played poker around a barrel used as a table. The civilian was Kim Miles, alias, Miles Harper, who had helped Bethel with her disguise. She was winning and not being very gracious about it.

"Read 'em and weep boys, kings over queens."

"Damn it you little weasel, that's four times in a row!" Mike Tyler, a farm boy from Iowa with an unshaven face slapped his cards down hard on the barrel top.

"Some of us are blessed by lady luck and some of us ain't." Miles laughed loudly.

Herschel Norris, a huge man with a bad temper glared at Harper. "I don't think it's got a damned thing to do with luck!"

"Yeah, I heard yer luck is uncommonly good around here." A sharpshooter named Browne added with a menacing growl in his tone.

Kim squirmed in her seat with an eye on the ample pot, but the scowls around the table keep her from scooping it up. "Come on fellas, this is just a game. No harm done. Hey, I won't even take the kitty. Keep it."She slowly slid off the crate used for a stool, snatched a handful of coins and darted from the tent. The icy streets made it hard to run, but Kim managed to disappear into an alley.

Walking close to a building for support Bethel made her way to the officer's quarters. The sound of fighting in the alley a few feet ahead of her alarmed Bethel who picked up the pace keeping one hand on the brick wall. The ice had melted and frozen back making traveling on it hazardous and slow.

Kim was around the corner being punched by the angry soldiers. She cried out and Bethel recognized the voice. The men were after the money, but Miles feared they would discover her secret if they kept rifling through her clothes and she fought back fiercely. She fell on her back and slid between the alley walls like a hockey puck as the soldiers kicked her back and forth.

Norris was red faced and pissed."You little shit! I want my goddamned money back!"

Browne grabbed her legs while Tyler sat on her legs. Norris started to search more ardently through her pockets promptly a barrage of curses from Miles. A figure appeared at the mouth of the alley in silhouette, the camp bonfires only casting a faint light. Bethel's rank was not visible to the fighters in the alley.

"This is none of your affair, just keep on moving!" Tyler commanded.

"That's a friend of mine you're kicking around which makes it my business." Bethel used her deepest voice.

Norris straightened up and approached the intruder. "You got one last chance to turn around and go."

Ignoring him Bethel took a few steps toward her friend. "Miles? Are you hurt?"

Kim pulled Tyler's legs out from under him and he landed flat on his buttocks. When Norris turned to see what happened, Bethel kicked him in the crotch. The action only made the large man angrier and punched her hard in the face making her lose her footing. Unable to grab anything to stop her fall, Bethel hit the ground hard with the back of her skull sending cracks rippling through the ice. She lay still where the light from the bonfires flickers on her medical insignia. At once the men realize that they have injured an officer. With eyes wide open Miles screamed. "You sons of bitches have had it now! You might as well desert."

A look of terror played on Norris' face before he took off toward the camp. Tyler and Browne followed, slipping and sliding until they reached the camp area where the ice was worn off. Kim Miles crawled over to Bethel where a pool of blood seeped out around her head like a crimson halo.
"Tandy! Oh shit, Tandy wake up!"

*************************

As George Erwin fought to break the Confederate fortifications known as Redoubt Number Five west of Nashville, a heavy fog hung over the field. The ground had thawed enough to making combat muddy and difficult in the afternoon. He felt a sudden odd sensation and developed a splitting headache that lasted through the evening. The news of his sister's condition had not yet reached him in the field, but George knew something had happened to Bethel.

*************************

Anna had convinced the orderlies responding to take the young injured assistant surgeon back to his quarters instead of the hospital, where her identity would surely be exposed. Bethel lay unconscious on the bed with the surgeon, Henry Crawford, sitting next to her.

"He has no pain response or any reaction to stimuli, I'm afraid that we must wait and see now." Crawford looked to Anna standing at the foot of the bed. "I've done all I can for now. Has his family been notified?"

"I've sent a letter to his aunt and uncle, but Tandy's cousin is on the front line somewhere, George Erwin." Anna pulled her shawl close around her.

Crawford rose from the rickety camp chair. "I need to get back, but you're doing as good a job as I could, Anna. I'll get word to George. Now don't get yourself in a depression. You know as well as I do that these men can pull out of the direst of situations." Anna shook her head sadly. "After everything he's been through, to be at death's door from a fall on the ice is a cruel joke."

The doctor patted Anna on the shoulder. "This war has been full of cruel jokes. Let's just hope we learn something from it all."

# Chapter Twenty Nine

George paced back and forth outside of Bethel's quarters with Kim Miles, who had dropped her male persona. She was an attractive woman and unrecognizable. Billie Jean walked Ella around a small camp fire as she clung tightly to a rag doll.

Miles, who was not comfortable in the dress, studied her shoes with a frown on her lips. "She was coming to my aid, you know. Me and my dumb stunts, but I never dreamed that Bethel would show up."

George plopped down on a stump. "Well, that just my sister, the knight in shining armor! Damn her. They arrested those three assholes, so at least we got that much."

"I don't understand Bethel or my own sister for that matter, but Bethel made sure that Anna saw some justice on this side of heaven and I got to respect her for that."

E lla stopped suddenly and looked up at Billie Jean. "Is Tandy going to heaven like Daddy?" The question caught the group off guard as the child rarely spoke.

Inside Lt. Tandy Scott's officer's quarters Jane Erwin sat near the bed with Anna Harold, her husband Bill leaned against a wall across from the small stove. Anna noticed that Jane would watch her and then quickly look away.

Turning to face Jane, Anna spoke softly. "I know this must be extremely difficult for you. I don't understand everything myself...I can tell you that if this very special person does not wake up, it will break my heart."

Anna began to sob and Jane takes Anna's hands. "Me too, dear. Me too."

Bill's eyes also fill with tears as he studied Bethel lying quiet. "She'd done the goddamnest things and lived through it without a scratch, then all this from a bump on the head. When she comes to I'll give her such an ass chewing."

*************************

On December 31, 1864 Dr. Crawford talked with Anna and Bill and Jane Erwin in his office at the Cumberland hospital. His expression was somber as he leaned over his desk with his hands gripped tightly together.

"The army wants to give Lt. Scott a medical discharge. I wish that I could tell you that I didn't think it was necessary, but at this point we have to face reality that even if he wakes up there will be brain damage."

"What sort of brain damage?" Anna spoke before Jane could get the words out.

"I expect some memory loss, maybe some loss of movement. He may have to learn to do something all over again. Injuries of the brain are the oddest of maladies in that they can send a man back to his infancy."

Jane squeezed her husband's hand as he stood next to her. "You mean like talking, he'll have to learn to speak again?"

Crawford nodded, his glasses slipping down his thin nose. "Yes, or walking or using his hands. You will also have to realize that Tandy may not ever wake up again. I am truly sorry to be the one to tell you this. Tandy is one of the best assistants I have had in this war. This is such a senseless tragedy."

Bill Erwin cleared his throat. "You're telling us to take him home then?"

"Yes sir. He'll have a full pension of course. I'm so sorry." The doctor rose to shack Bill's hand.

The walk back to the officer's quarters is a silent one with each of them struggling with their own thoughts and feelings. Anna's face is full of strain as she approaches the small shack she calls home with Bethel. Bill and Jane are several yards behind her speaking quietly between them. Anna fears they will take their daughter home and she will never seen Bethel again. She couldn't blame them. Anna never would have believed before the war that she could fall in love with another woman.

"Anna, could we talk with you?" Jane stepped up behind her.

"Why yes, of course." Anna fights tears.

"We're just simple country folk and there's a whole lot we don't know about the world, but we know one thing. You and Ella mean a great deal to Bethel and we don't think it would do her any good at all to wake up and find you not there."

Bill watched as he held his hat over his belt buckle. "It's going to be shock enough to find herself back home after four years of military life."

Tears rolled down Anna's cheeks. "You are just as wonderful as Tandy says you are. Excuse me, I mean Bethel."

Bill approached Anna and put an arm around her shoulders. "Thanks much, but Jane's mother sat us down and gave us a good talking to. Grandma Carter knows a lot about people and human nature and she helped us understand more than we did."

"Lord, my mother has seen much more in this world than I had realized." Jane chuckled.

"Sometimes that old woman makes me feel like a piker." Bill put his hat back on as a cold breeze whipped through the compound. "We'd be pleased to have you come home with us." Jane offered.

Anna looked up at the heavy gray clouds that seemed only moments away from dumping more snow and ice on the already dreary city. She nodded in agreement.

## Chapter Thirty
Erwin Homestead in Tennessee
Late winter 1865


By the middle of January Bethel was still in a coma. She lay still as a winter rain storm settled over the area. All through the thunder and lightning she remained dormant, unlike before the war when the teenaged girl would crawl out onto the porch roof and let the rain hit her face. Flashes of lightning illuminated her face as Anna sat in a rocking chair by the window watching the raging weather outside. Grandma Carter had no doubt that Bethel would wake up as she said there were several states of stupor. Since her granddaughter cold sip soup and water and had begun to twitch and moan, Grandma was certain Bethel would recover.

The sobbing of a child pulled Anna's attention away from the window. Ella had always been afraid of storms and she climbed up into her mother's lap. Anna patted the child's back and hummed a lullaby for several minutes as her own eyes battled sleep. Suddenly a loud crack shattered the air as a bolt of lightning hit a nearby tree. Anna jerked from surprise and Ella screamed as Bethel sat upright in the bed and yelled.

Bethel then stared at Anna wide- eyed. "Who the hell are you?"

Anna was speechless for several seconds then hollered for Bill and Jane Erwin who came rushing in wearing their long johns and night gown, bleary eyed from the sudden separation from sleep. Jane took in a long breath.

"Well, I'll be damned." Bill smiled.

"What? Why are you all in my room and who are they?" Bethel looked bewildered and her heart pounded against her sternum. "I'm really hungry. Is there any bread jam?"

Grandma Carter had been staying with the Erwins to monitor Bethel's condition. She emerged from the bedroom down the hall and peered into the room. "There's plenty of time for talk. Help her down the stairs and we'll all have a little snack."

Bethel was weak, but able to stand by herself and refused the help. Years of running, hunting and fishing in the mountains had kept her muscles toned even before military service. Her features looked puzzled as Ella smiled and waved shyly at Bethel.

"You'll let us help you down the stairs, child. I insist." Grandma ordered sternly.

Sensing that something was not right Bethel complied and held onto her father's arm down the wide staircase. "I'm really fine. I don't understand why you're treating me like a baby."

While Bill and Jane lit lanterns in the kitchen, Grandma fetched the bread and strawberry jam. Anna tossed another log on the smoldering fire. When they were all settled around the table with bread and coffee, Joy came down the stairs and into the kitchen. "So, you decided to wake up? Good, I'm tired of doing your chores. Can I have some too?"

"What do you mean, wake up?" Bethel asked suspiciously.

"You had a blow to the head and you've been laying in a stupor for some time. What do you remember last?" Grandma asked gently.

Bethel peered at the ceiling, her eyes rolling from one stain to another as she thought. "Me and George were talking about the joining up posters in town. He was thinking of doing some fightin' for the Rebs." The faces at the table were somber. "Did he? Did George join the army?"

"Yes, he and Tim both joined up. You don't remember that?" Bill asked her.

Bethel shook her head. "No, I sure don't. How long they been gone?"

Bill looked to Grandma Carter, afraid to tell her, but she nodded.
"Bethel, they left over three years ago."
Sitting dumbfounded Bethel was silent. "I've been asleep that long?"
She pondered in a low voice.
Jane put an arm around her daughter's shoulders. "No, child, you hit
your head only a few weeks ago.
"I don't remember George and Tim leaving town. Are you a friend
of George's?" Bethel addressed Anna.
With a heavy heart Anna nodded slightly. "Yes, I know
George and Tim…" She stopped as Grandma Carter sent her a
cautionary glance.
Bill sensed that too much conversation might wear the already
weaken Bethel down. "There's plenty of time for chatting later. Let's
not do too much now."
Grandma Carter agreed with him and told everyone they
should finish up as it was the middle of the night. Bethel studied
Anna Harold's sad face and knew something was amiss. Had George
died and nobody wanted to tell her?
"I am rather tired, I guess lying down would be the best thing, even
though I just got up!"
A week later Bethel sat in the porch swing watching Anna
hang out the wash. Ella sat next to her holding onto to Bethel's hand,
which did not surprise her as children had always liked her.
Grandma Carter rocked in a chair nearby and embroidered.
Gradually, the family had given Bethel information about the last
four years. She knew that she had joined the army and worked as a
surgeon. Her parents thought it best that Bethel remember marrying
Anna on her own, though Grandma Carter doubted it would be that
traumatic for her granddaughter.
Ella stared up at Bethel with a serious expression. "What happened
to your whiskers? You don't look right anymore."
"Sometimes we all need a change child, like putting on a clean
dress." Grandma Carter jumped in.
The child accepted the response with "oh."
"I can't believe that I lost four years of my life, and from the sound
of it, the most interesting years. The last thing I recall is me and
George walking down the street with a recruiting poster." She
smiled, pleased with herself. "I really doctored people during the
war!"

Anna picked up the laundry basket then sat on the porch steps. "You sure did, as Lt. Tandy Scott, assistant surgeon in the Union army."

"I accept what you all tell me, but for all I know myself, George is just off hunting somewhere without me. I still don't know who you are, Anna." Bethel said softly.

"All in good time, Beth. Not too much at once!" Grandma Carter slapped her knee.

Ella scowled. "His name ain't Beth! He's Tandy and he's my new daddy. You're dumb!"

The little girl slipped off the porch and ran over to play with Ellen and Joy who chased around a new calf in the yard. Bethel looked to Anna with a pained expression.

Grandma chuckled. "And a little child shall lead them!"

Bethel blushed and picked at her fingernails. "I have a feeling that I out did myself this time."

"That is an understatement. Why don't you two take a walk and I'll watch the young'uns."

Anna stood up and offered her hand to Bethel. "We do have much to talk about."

\*\*\*\*\*\*\*\*\*\*\*\*\*\*\*\*\*\*\*\*\*\*\*\*

Two weeks later Anna packed her suitcase and Ella threw a furious fit about leaving the Erwin farm. It was causing all of them a great deal of pain for Anna to remain there and her own parents in Boston expected her home. Bethel still had no memory of her or the war.

"I don't want to go! I wanna stay with Grandpa Bill and Grandma Jane!"

"So do I, sweetheart, but we don't always get what we want." For Anna, Tandy Scott may as well have died in the war. She was a widow for the second time.

"Is Tandy coming too?"

Anna knelt down next to her daughter. "Honey, Tandy was very sick and he doesn't remember us. We are strangers to him. Oh, I know you don't understand. How could you when I do not?"

Shouting and whistling makes Anna run into the hallway and peer down the stairs. The Erwin's are dancing around and hugging. Bill saw her and told Anna that George had made it home and he had a girl with him. She ran to Joy's room and looked out the window to see George limping down the path through the pasture with a cane. Billie Jean held onto his other arm.

As the rest of the family ran out the front door Bethel emerged from the barn. Anna rushed down the porch steps to hug her sister.

"This is such a wonderful surprise! George how are you?" Anna asked as studied the cane.

George's unshaven face made him appear like a tramp. "Well, I won't be winning any foot races, but I'm still breathing." He paused. "How is Bethel?"

Anna let out a sigh, her pain obvious. "She doesn't remember anything at all. As far as Bethel is concerned she never left this farm."

"I'm sorry, Anna. We've all been through so much together." George looked to Billie Jean.

"At least we are all still alive, Anna. There is time for Bethel to heal too…"

The Erwin clan surrounded them with beaming faces and cheerful voices. Anna backed away to let them have their moment of happiness. She felt sorry for Bethel who seemed so lost and stood near the corral. Anna went to her and took her former spouses' hand. "Let's go greet George and Billie Jean together?" Anna suggested. Bethel's eyes were kind. She looked at Anna much the same as she had when they were Mr. and Mrs. Tandy Scott. Somewhere in Bethel's heart she still remembered their past relationship.

"Of course, we can, this is very happy day after all." Bethel smiled and guided Anna to their returning siblings.

\*\*\*\*\*\*\*\*\*\*\*\*\*\*\*\*\*\*\*\*\*\*

Two nights later when George and Billie Jean were entertaining the family with war stories around the table, Bethel sat in the living room before the fire staring at the flames while her mother darned socks. Anna came down the stairs with her suitcases in tow and placed them near the front door. Jane put down the mending and asked Anna if she was leaving. Before she could answer her sister saw the suitcases from the other room and rushed up to her.

"You can't! George and me are getting married this weekend. Anna don't go now!" Billie Jean stopped herself before reminding Anna that she had stood up for her.

"Please stay a little while longer." Jane's voice bore a motherly tone. "At least for the wedding."

Anna's face had a haunted appearance. Mildred Carter had just come out of the kitchen wiping her hands on a dish towel. She walked over to Anna and put an arm around her shoulders. "I'd like to walk a bit in the night air, why don't you keep me company?" Anna turned to Bethel, desperately wanting to see Lt. Scott, but she only seemed sad and lost. Jane nodded that she should go with grandma. "I could use some fresh air."

At the well Anna splashed cold water on her face. The night sky was filled with bright stars, the very same ones she had walked under when Tandy loved her.

"Don't wash those tears away, you got very right to cry." Mildred took Anna's arm and walked her toward the barn.

"I'm in hell, Mildred. No one seems to see it."

"I think you've earned the right to call me grandma, and they do, they just don't know what to say." The night air was colder than Mildred had figured and she pulled her shawl tight around her. Anna leaned into Mildred, clutching the older woman's arm. "Billie is so happy, so was I such a short time ago."

Mildred pulled Anna close. "Let it all out, child."

"The person I loved died in that alley. It hurts so much to look at Beth and not have her remember me. What am I even saying? It could never have been, we were just living a dream. It's better this way."

Stepping back with her hands firmly on Anna's shoulders Mildred's tone was firm, but gentle. "I don't believe that and neither do you! You have a right to grieve. You're a sweet lady, Anna and none of us want to see you go, including Bethel."

"How can I stay, grandma? I still love Tandy Scott and that person is gone. It isn't fair to Beth either. This must all be very hard on her."

"Beth is one tough cookie, you should know. The person you loved is still here, just give her time. As for you two having a life together being a dream, let me tell you that the world is a varied place. You would not be the first women to live as a married couple, oh don't look so surprised. I've been treating folk in these hills for forty years and you can't imagine the things I've seen. You're love for Beth is far from the strangest phenomenon, trust me!"

"I don't know if I can stay here, it is just too painful. I'm tired of being strong, grandma."

"Do one more brave thing then and stay for your sister's wedding. You know as sure as I do that it won't be a happy day if you and Ella are off on a train."

On the darkened porch behind the climbing rose bush, Bethel had been listening to their conversation. Anna was beautiful, gentle and sweet. How could she not remember being married to a woman like that? What could she do to help mend her brain? When she saw the two women turn toward the house Bethel slipped back inside.

## Chapter Thirty-One


The wedding was planned for two days later on Saturday. George had always wanted an outdoor wedding on the hill overlooking the house, but winter still clung fiercely to eastern Tennessee. He also wanted his sister standing by him as she had during the war, but he relented and asked his father to be his best man. Reverend Wilkes had moved on and another preacher would preside, David Harrison. Anna would be Billie Jean's matron of honor. The marriage vows would be exchanged in the Erwin living room with a small reception afterwards. The weather would prevent anything more elaborate.

The snow and ice also kept the children from attending school. Joy took a glass of milk upstairs to her room where she would read from the primer. The attic stairs were down near her bedroom, so Joy placed the milk next to her bed then ascended the stairs to see who was up there. At the top of the stairs she saw Bethel sitting on the floor with her army uniform in her lap. She went back down and retrieved a bundle of letters from her room then returned to the attic.

"You sent this to me from Corinth." Joy handed her sister a photograph.

Bethel looked up. "I did?"  It was a picture of Bethel in uniform after she had been promoted to Sergeant Major.

"I saved all your letters, even though we used to fight all the time. You changed when you went off to war. You told me about Anna, but nobody else. It made me feel grown up and I kept your secret. I haven't told anyone that I knew all along." She grinned. "Everybody thinks I'm such a goody two shoes, but I fooled them!"

"You didn't tell anybody after all this time? Damn it, I want to remember so badly. I really had the gumption to do it." Bethel seemed amazed at her own audacity.

"Why don't you read through these letters and maybe it will help. I need to read my assignment for the night, Ma makes us do school work at home since we can't go."

"I know, I recall things that far back." She watches Joy begin to go down the stairs. "Thanks for keeping your mouth shut and for saving the letters. Hey would you put the stairs back up, I don't want Ella trying to climb up here." Joy waved and disappeared through the hole in the attic floor.

For the next two nights Bethel read through her letters and studied photographs in the attic until the early morning hours. On Friday evening she even put on the uniform in hopes it would jangle some memory from her brain. Never had she ever been so angry at herself and cried in frustration. She fell fast asleep amid the war memorabilia.

The next morning George stood straight and tall in his bedroom as Bill buttoned the high collar and put a fancy knot in the black tie. "Thanks, Pa. Where the hell is Bethel? Has anybody seen her?"

"I haven't. Let me holler down at yer Ma."

Bill started for the door, but his son brushed past him to the master bedroom where the women were dressing Billie Jean. George knocked on the door then opened it a crack.

"George Erwin don't you be looking in here it's bad luck!" Grandma Carter shouted at him.

"Grandma, have you seen Bethel?" His voice was mixed with irritation and worry.

"No, now that I think of it I haven't. Has anybody seen her today?" Mildred looked around at Anna, Ella, Joy and Billie Jean.

"She was in the attic last night holding up her uniform, but I left her up there and went to bed. Beth has been doing that a lot. Anna have you seen her?" Joy looked anxiously at Anna.

"No. Her bed was empty, but I didn't think much about it as she has been getting up to milk the cows." Anna fitted Billie Jean's veil. George frowned then shut the door. He pulled down the attic stairs and then fast as he could with a bum leg climbed up to where he could see Bethel sacked out on the floor.

"Bethel! Bethel, what the hell are ya doing?"

His sister lay on her stomach under the lower part of the roof. Letters and photographs littered the area and Bethel was wearing her uniform. George's loud voice startled her award and she smacked the back of her head hard on a wood beam. She moaned and held the wound to ease the pain. Crawling on all fours to a trunk Bethel pulled herself up on it.

She squeezed her eyes shut to stop the dizziness and fought the nausea that rushed up suddenly. Bethel's hand felt wet and opened her eyes to find it crimson with blood. Visions begin to come to her of Shiloh, being shot by Neukirk and blood oozing from Tim's ear. Panic seized her and she grabbed the kepi near the trunk and pulled it on.

"Oh shit, my patients! I can't be here I have patients. I am in so much trouble!"

George saw her bearing down on him and backed down the stairs right before she came clumping down them. He stood outside her bedroom watching a confused Bethel look around. When she saw him dressed up Bethel made a funny sound.

"Where are you going?" She grinned.

"I'm getting married in two hours, what the hell are you doing?" George asked her as she stood there in the Union army uniform. The racket brought Bill and the women out into the hallway. They stared at Bethel not quite knowing what to think. Anna's face lit up at the familiar sight of Bethel in uniform.

"Lt. Scott?" Anna asked timidly.

"Anna? What's going on? I shouldn't be here…" Bethel felt sick and leaned against the wall.

George looked her straight in the eyes. "You remember us joining the army?"

"Why wouldn't I? Last thing I know is I was saving Miles' ass in that fight. What I am doing here?" She snorted as she looked George up and down. "So, who was dumb enough to say yes?"

George and Bill helped Bethel down the stairs. "Billie Jean, now who else I have been courting?"
She grimaced. "Oh my skull hurts."
George laughed. "Serves ya right." He joked with his sister, but was thrilled that she seemed to be recovered.

The women followed to the ground floor where George led Bethel to a chair in the kitchen. Mildred wanted to study her granddaughter's condition in private.
"We're all standing around here like a bunch of gawking heifers! Let's give her some room. We still have a wedding to get ready for! Go on now, shoo!"

Anna gently removed the kepi from Bethel's bloody hair as Mildred went to the pitcher and poured water onto a rag. The cut was sharp, but not deep like the first wound.
"I smacked my head upstairs." Bethel looked up at Anna who smiled and nodded then pulled a chair around to face her.
Mildred gently wiped the matted hair as she studied Bethel's eyes for any sign of brain injury. "You need to quit smacking that skull of yours!" Bethel seemed puzzled. "You cracked your head in Nashville and loss your senses, you didn't know Anna or that you had been in the army. Do you remember now?"

"How long have I been home?" She asked in disbelief.
"Nearly three weeks, with the first two being in a stupor. The last week you woke up, but had no recall of the war or anything right before leaving on that train." Mildred took Bethel's hands. "Are you alright?"
"Except for the headache, I think so." Bethel looked at Anna. "I'm so sorry! It must have been terrible for you. How could I forget my grass widow? "
Mildred winked at Anna when she seemed confused.
"I'm fine. The wedding is in two hours. If you feel like joining us I'll bring a change of clothes down." Anna offered.
George popped back into the kitchen after overhearing them. "I want ya to wear your uniform and stand up for me. Pa doesn't mind."

"Oh, I don't know…what would people around here think?"
Bethel shook her head involuntarily making her frown from the pain.
"Ain't nobody here but us, and I don't give an owl's fart what that preacher thinks!" George grinned.

Jane smacked her son on the shoulder as she came up behind him. "George Erwin, don't be talking like that."

"She don't have to stand; Bethel can sit in a chair next to me." George smiled at being chastised. "Besides you owe me the favor Tandy Scott!"

Two hours later in the Erwin living room George and Billie Jean faced Reverend Harrison with Bethel and Anna beside them. Bill and Jane stood together close by and when Bill shook his head over his daughter in uniform his mother in law elbowed him. Ella clapped her hands in the excitement of being the flower girl. "I now pronounce you husband and wife."

A beaming George lifted her veil and kissed his new bride, who then tossed the bouquet over her head. Joy laughed as she caught it and curtsied.

"Everyone to the kitchen for cake and ice cream!" Jane shouted. Since the weather, the economy and the war made a honeymoon I mpractical, George promised Billie Jean a trip in the future to make up for it. Instead of running off to enjoy a few days alone, the newlyweds ventured into the kitchen to savor the four layer cake that Jane made for them.

"Reverend, are you going to join us?" Jane asked, already knowing his response.

"Why that's the best part of being a preacher Mrs. Erwin!" Harrison rubbed his ample stomach and followed her into the kitchen.

Anna started after them until Bethel reached out and grabbed her hand. "Talk a walk with me first."

"You do know it is snowing outside?" Anna responded looking through the large bay window in the living room.

Bethel shrugged. "With all the weather we've lived in the past few years, who cares about a few snowflakes?" She got up from the chair and went to the front closet to fetch their coats and gloves. "I have something I want to show you."

The two women walked through the front yard past the barn toward the path in the woods. Bill could see them from the kitchen doorway. "Bethel's smart like us men, we show up for the eatin' and then disappear for the dishwashin'."

Mildred peeked around him and saw Bethel take Anna's arm with the snow swirling around them. "Traditions change, Bill Erwin, as you should be more than aware with a daughter like Bethel."

The woods were quiet, nature muffled by the white blanket that grew slowly thicker around them. For the first time since leaving for Nashville in 1861 Bethel marveled at the landscape without the sounds of bullets and cannon balls screeching past. There were no wounded screaming for help, no acrid blue smoke choking the air, no blood tinted snow and the creek below them ran clear. She felt a sudden rush of shame for ever being glad the war started.
A narrow path curved off the trail and Bethel steered them down it. Anna sensed sadness in Bethel and pulled her close as they approached a cliff that jutted out toward the Erwin house far below.

"It's beautiful up here, but I could have waited to see it." Anna joked.

Bethel responded by breaking off a pine branch and using it as a broom to sweep off a lump in the snow a few feet off the clearing. Stepping through the snow Anna joined Bethel who stood staring down at a light colored stone on the ground. The engraving was faded, but the name "Tandy Scott" was still readable.
"He was a Scotsman who was struck by lightning while playing bagpipes up here. He was an odd duck like me, so I figured it was a good name to use."

Anna pondered the thought of anyone playing bagpipes in a thunderstorm."He must have been fond of the drink."
Bethel snickered. "Probably. I used to look out my window at this spot up here. Even when the clouds fill the valley this place rises up like a vanquishing warrior or at least that the way I used to think of it. I've changed a lot since then." She paused. "I want to bury Bethel Erwin."

Alarmed Anna turned her head swiftly toward Bethel, who never had seemed suicidal to her.

As if she read Anna's mind Bethel shook her head. "Not for real, I don't want to ever live as a woman again. I can't be myself and do that Anna.   I have no intention of ever living as Bethel Erwin again"
"The months you spent in a coma were horrible for me, but not as terrible as the time when you didn't know who I was. I thought my heart would crumble into a thousand pieces every time you looked at me with someone else's eyes."

B ethel hugged Anna tightly. "I promise to never do that to you again. How could I have forgotten you? What a fool I am."

"You're not a fool, you were severely injured. I would like to give that Kim Miles a thrashing though." Anna buried her face in Bethel's shoulder as snowflakes fell on the dark blue uniform. Her love for another woman was against all she had been taught. Everyone she knew back in Boston would condemn her for it, but the idea of living without her was impossible.

"I love you, Anna. I don't know how we'd manage it, but I don't want to make a life without you." Bethel kissed Anna's warm forehead.

After a few seconds Anna pulled back with an enlightened expression. "I am legally married to Tandy Scott. No one ever suspected you of being a woman before even in the most intimate of circumstances, so why would they now? Especially, if you would wear that mustache again, you're quite handsome with it you know."
"You have any idea of how itchy that spirit gum can get?" She laughed, and then grew serious. "If anyone ever found out we'd be humiliated and run out of whatever town we lived in."

"My family lives in Boston where there is a good medical school. You could go there to become a doctor and then we could move where ever we wanted to go." Anna's eyes sparkled with the belief that they could actually do it.

"I hear they don't have nearly enough doctors in California. Dr. and Mrs. Scott, can you imagine it?" Bethel's lips slipped into a crooked grin.

"I don't have to imagine it, sweetheart, I've lived it and I want to keep living it."

"I'd love to be a real, official doctor…your family wouldn't mind my coming with you?" The snow was piling up on Bethel's shoulders and the cold had tinted her cheeks pink.

Anna took her arm and turned Bethel around for the trip down the wooded hill. "How could they object to my husband coming home with me to attend medical school? I can tell you that the prestige is what my mother craves. We'll be fine and I sense that we have a long and exciting future ahead of us."


The End

www.ingramcontent.com/pod-product-compliance
Lightning Source LLC
Chambersburg PA
CBHW071718140626
46557CB00012B/947